WEEDING FOR EISENHOWER

Stories

T.D. JOHNSTON

Winner of the International Book Award for
Friday Afternoon and Other Stories

"T.D. Johnston is a literary conjuror par excellence. Reading *Weeding for Eisenhower* is like stepping into virtual reality. You experience the lives of his remarkable characters not just with them, but from inside them. Their struggles, fears, loves and learnings become your own. Your heart beats with their pulse. This is storytelling at its finest." —*Marjorie Brody, multiple award-winning author of* **Twisted**

∾

"The beauty of T.D. Johnston's new collection of short stories, *Weeding for Eisenhower*, is this. You have no idea where Johnston is going to take you. But when you get there, you always say the same thing: Thanks. And you always do the same thing. You go back to the beginning and read it again." —*Tom Sorensen, award-winning columnist,* **The Charlotte Observer**

∾

"T.D. Johnston is not a writer to be trusted. The world he shows you may seem familiar, but across these stories about race, class, childhood and memory falls a shadow, a sense of menace, sometimes an overt threat. And just when you've figured out that where there's smoke, there's mirrors, he'll surprise you with an unexpected affirmation, a reunion, a benediction, maybe an email from God. *Weeding for Eisenhower* challenges and rewards on every page." —*Jon Tuttle, author of* **The Trustus Collection**

∾

"Light versus Dark. Good versus Evil. Truth versus Lies. Sanity versus Madness. The thin line that separates these dichotomies threads its way through these beautifully written stories of modern America, showing us time after time Johnston's keen ability to illuminate the human condition. And if you are like me, you will come away from reading these often surprising tales with a renewed optimism that there is more that connects us than separates us." —*Ray Morrison, author of* **In a World of Small Truths**

~

"T.D. Johnston's *Weeding for Eisenhower* is a tour de force. At once engaging and enthralling, this multifaceted collection allows your mind to wander through its cavernous halls, a book that calls you to attention, leaving you thinking long after you've left its pages. If you want stories that stick with you, this book is for you." —*Katie Piccirillo Sherman, author of* **They Always Wave Goodbye**

~

"In *Weeding for Eisenhower*, T.D. Johnston has done nothing less than defy gravity. At the top of his game with his award-winning debut collection *Friday Afternoon and Other Stories*, he aims even higher in this second work, and then delivers on the challenge. Things in some T.D. Johnston stories are exactly what they seem, until they are not, the power of the story slamming home in a delicious twist. In others, we know we had best strap in tight from the very first. In these eighteen tales, this modern master of the short form reminds us why we love the short story." —*John W. MacIlroy, author of* **Whatever Happens, Probably Will**

~

"The American short story has no better friend than T.D. Johnston, whose second collection runs the gamut of the form's possibilities. Earnest children, desperate men, and troubled women narrate a remarkable range of lived experience in tales set in the present, the recent past, and in other eras. Common to all these stories is a knowing edge that binds them together. For Johnston, terror, folly, and great affection lie adjacent in every human heart." —*Richard Hawley, award-winning author of* **The Headmaster's Papers**

∾

"There's a certain feeling you get while reading a short story from T.D. Johnston: It's a comfort in knowing a story is in this writer's capable hands. He's the type of author who's going to invite you in, offer you a cup of tea and some good conversation, before he pulls the rug out from under you and leaves you head over heels when you least expect it. His new collection, *Weeding for Eisenhower,* is a master class on how to deliver stories that grab you from the first page and don't let you go until long after reading." —*D.G. Bracey, Author and Professor of Creative Writing, Coastal Carolina University*

∾

"Writing of this caliber can remove us from our reality as we navigate the complex journeys of a variety of multi-dimensional characters whose hearts ultimately begin to beat alongside our own. This collection is masterful from a craft perspective, yes, but it also illuminates our collective story—the struggles and realizations that bind us but are all too easy to forget." —*Jen Knox, author of* **Resolutions: A Family in Stories** *(AUXmedia, a division of Aquarius Books)*

∾

"T.D. Johnston is not only one of the country's foremost champions of the short story, but one of the genre's most skilled practitioners as well. In his latest collection, *Weeding for Eisenhower,* we find ourselves in the company of a writer who has a sensitive finger on the pulse of the world we live in right now and its often polarized and bewildering strangeness. But Johnston's stories go unerringly to the core of what is solid and eternal, and in doing so bring a semblance of order to our fractured reality. These stories will chill your blood, warm your heart, slap you wide awake, touch you with gentle sorrow, and make you laugh out loud. Enjoy the ride!" —*Douglas Campbell, winner of the **Able Muse Write Prize for Fiction***

∾

"Some will call 'Weeding for Eisenhower' a collection of short stories, but that fails to recognize the true nature of these superlative fictions. Properly, this is oral storytelling written down with the honesty and urgency of a writer at the top of his form. From a father telling his adult daughter a story over the phone, to a couple asking each other a barrage of questions, Johnston invokes the spoken word with such imagination and nuance that characters and stories come to life with little authorial intrusion. In the process, Johnston stakes a claim as a master of spoken and written storytelling." —*William R. Hincy, author of **Without Expiration**, named one of the Best Books of 2020 by Kirkus Reviews*

∾

"This second collection from T.D. Johnston, a torch-bearer of the American short story, is varied, contemporary, and timeless. His range is amazing: narrators a broad spectrum of men and women, characters and points of view from slaves to Covid-era white boys, understanding fathers and cheating husbands and delusional wives, a girl of seven, and many more... even an email from God. Moral and immoral and amoral, these ideas come up in every story in this fine collection. Classic in structure and depth, with the arrival again and again of the unexpected, these tales are completely and terrifically original, yet pay tribute to masters like Poe, O.Henry, O'Connor, and Carver. This book is loaded with technically brilliant stories that should be taught in the prep schools and high schools Johnston writes of. Enjoy!" —*Gregg Cusick, winner of the* **Lorian Hemingway Short Story Prize**

~

"T.D. Johnston's newest collection *Weeding for Eisenhower* is delightfully eclectic, has expansive variety, offers incredible energy and range, and is deeply inspiring. At this buffet, there is something for every reader." —*Niles Reddick, author of* **Reading the Coffee Grounds**

~

"I have long been a fan of T.D. Johnston's layered and cerebral short stories. *Weeding for Eisenhower* is another jewel in the crown of an author who simply has nothing left to prove, and will delight his readers, whether long-time fans or the newly-initiated. He writes in historical, current and visionary contexts with equal ease, exploring good and evil, love and hate, dignity and degradation, freedom and subjugation, learning and ignorance, omission and commission. Some stories are lighter-hearted, others are decidedly not; every one of them deserves to be re-read—again and again—to unpack all the levels of meaning. This is one rollercoaster of a read. And we have come to expect nothing less from T.D. Johnston." —*Jayne Adams, author of the forthcoming short story collection* **For All the Right Seasons**

❦

TABLE OF CONTENTS

*This book is dedicated
to the memory of
Bob and Ruth Johnston.*

"They say, best men are moulded out of faults;
And, for the most, become much more the better
For being a little bad."

—William Shakespeare, *Measure for Measure*

"Without Contraries is no progression. Attraction and
Repulsion, Reason and Energy, Love and Hate,
are necessary to Human existence."

—William Blake, *The Marriage of Heaven and Hell*

A REAL MOTHER

✳ ✳ ✳

Three weeks after Kerry Tisdale graduated from college, she took the trip to Europe her parents awarded her as a graduation gift, with a second week added for making Phi Beta Kappa. While in Paris, then Tuscany, then Rome, then Venice, then back west to London before flying home to Atlanta, she enjoyed great food and drink, visited many historic sites, observed classic works of art and architecture, and fell in love with a handsome man named Khalid, whom she met on her second tour of the Louvre. Khalid was an artist. He was twenty-seven years old, had studied at the Sorbonne, was currently trying his hand at Monet-style impressionism, and was brown. Khalid was also Muslim, but Kerry tried not to think about that when they made love in Khalid's small but well-appointed apartment above a quaint café the night before she left for Italy. By not thinking about that, Kerry invited Khalid to accompany her to Venice and then London, an invitation Khalid accepted. While in Venice Khalid painted a Venetian canal scene that Kerry insisted Monet would proudly have hung on his dining-room wall.

Kerry Tisdale was the only child of very Republican parents, and the fourth Republican grandchild of very Republican grandparents. The family's Republican loyalty was so powerful that all members of the living generations of Tisdales and Harrisons (Kerry's mother being from Houston) voted in 2016 for a man they each loathed, as told in commiseration that Thanksgiving. Kerry's membership in the College Republicans for the past four years had been expected by Tisdales and Harrisons alike, and she did not disappoint.

In London, on the eve of her return flight to America, Kerry considered for the first time that Khalid, a magnificent artist and generous lover, a kind man with a dry sense of humor that Kerry could picture making her laugh on their fiftieth anniversary, would be a problem on the other side of the Atlantic.

So at dawn on the final Friday of her graduation trip, while Khalid slept after a night of passionate lovemaking at a London hotel, Kerry took a cab to Heathrow Airport. Later, while enjoying surf and turf for lunch in first class miles above the deepest trenches of the Atlantic, Kerry unfriended and blocked Khalid on Facebook. She deleted the selfies of the two of them which Khalid had posted on her timeline last night before opening their second bottle of wine. She regretted having to block him, but she wanted to avoid the hurt of seeing his smiling face again. There had been zero likes on the photos when she deleted them. She was in the clear. When the in-flight movie about a brave female DEA agent fizzled into mindless action after about forty minutes, she dozed off and on for the remainder of the flight to Atlanta.

Back at her parents' home in Buckhead, Kerry began to pack for her move to Memphis, where on July 1st she would begin her fast-track sales management career with one of America's leading consumer-goods companies. For six months she would learn the strategic ground-level relationships with supermarket chains and big-box retailers, before being promoted into brand management if all went well. A month ago she had located a nice two-bedroom apartment on a home-hunting visit with her mother. Furniture was being delivered on June 29th, so she had about ten days left at home to spend with her friends and family.

On June 26th, while in Midtown for an evening with friends, she saw a young man who looked a lot like Khalid. The man was wearing a tight grey tee shirt and khaki shorts, and was laughing with two young black women in seventies-style halter tops. An image flashed of Khalid painting in Venice, then an earlier vision of Khalid leaning in to kiss her for the first time while they sat out a rainstorm with café crème and warm croissants under a table umbrella next to a cobblestone side street in Paris. Suddenly she desired the man at the bar with the two haltered women. She fought the urge to steal him, battled the greater urge to remember Khalid, and drank another Fat Tire toast to the brilliant futures she and her companions each individually possessed. The world really was their oyster. It really was.

The morning of June 28th arrived too fast. Kerry wished she had a few more days to transition into the oyster part of her life, but furniture was arriving in Memphis tomorrow, and she had to be there with the key she would pick up from the apartment complex's manager this afternoon at five. She had an early-morning breakfast with her mom and dad, savoring her mom's poached eggs for what absurdly felt like the last time. Sitting in sudden sad silence with them, she found herself wishing she had said goodbye to Khalid, or that she had somehow left the door open for something more. She pictured him with another woman, maybe not this soon but soon still. Or maybe even right now, locked in rolling ecstatic passion. The concept bothered her, as did the awful certainty that the latter was the reality. If she wanted him, so did other women. They would have him, and he would have them. For the first time in her life, a man Kerry Tisdale dumped was a man Kerry Tisdale wanted back.

But just as suddenly she knew that the fling was just that, merely and only that, a dalliance with a man who would not be welcome at the Church of the Apostles, where she would get married because that's what her parents expected of her. Kerry valued practicality. No, she thought, actually she valued pragmatism, recognizing the distinction as she sipped her orange juice on this goodbye morning. She had learned much about the usefulness of pragmatism in her minor field of political science, which interested her far more than her major study in economics. She had pragmatically made the only viable decision in London, fortunately after satisfying and therefore removing the temporary temptations of desire, one last delicious time, an hour before tiptoeing to the hotel-room door.

Kerry excused herself from the dining table and went upstairs to brush her teeth and pack toiletries into her final suitcase. Everything else was in her car, a late-model grey Volvo SUV that her father had researched and chosen for its high crash rating and durability. As she brushed her teeth, she began to feel sick to the stomach. Too much beer last night, she knew. The feeling passed. She examined her shoulder-length dark brown hair in the mirror, ran her fingers through the lush locks, contemplated makeup while knowing she didn't need it, and spit in the sink after swishing for thirty seconds. She put her toothbrush and toothpaste in her toiletries bag and turned to exit the bathroom when the sick feeling returned. It was nausea. This time she stepped to the toilet, descended to her knees, and threw up her poached eggs and English muffin. *Great*, she thought as she wiped her mouth with toilet paper. *Sick for the endless drive to Memphis.*

She did not know then that she was pregnant. Knowing that she was pregnant would have made for a particularly rough drive to Memphis, particularly because Kerry's family was particularly opposed to abortion, their particular opposition to abortion being due to their particular position, shared by many, that abortion was murder. Kerry had said so herself at more than one meeting of particularly like-minded College Republicans. So it was good that she did not know she was pregnant during her drive to Memphis. It was good that she did not have to consider that the baby's father was a kind, funny, artistic black Muslim man named Khalid living on the other side of the big pond the day before her furniture would arrive, and two days before she would start her career in a world that was her oyster. By the time she and the Volvo crossed over the north Georgia border into Tennessee en route toward I-40, the nausea was a thing of the past, the Bose was blasting variously from fifteen pre-set satellite channels, and Khalid had moved on from her mind, replaced by her excitement about the tan velvet living-room furniture, the beautiful maple dining suite, and the king-size bed that she would break in tomorrow night before starting her new life as a budding corporate executive-in-training.

Pulling into a McDonald's off the highway outside of Chattanooga, Kerry parked and entered the fast-food restaurant, stretching her legs rather than sit in the drive-through lane. While in line at the one open cash register, the nausea returned. She left the line, hurried to the women's restroom, and discovered that the lone stall was occupied. She was annoyed. She cleared her throat, not to be obvious but to sound sick, which she was. Then she whispered, in case the occupant of the stall was oblivious, "Oh my God, I'm going to be so sick." She pronounced the last word slowly, and waited for the woman in the stall to respond with an obligatory "I'm so sorry" and an emphatic roll of the toilet-paper holder.

Silence.

"Excuse me," Kerry said. "But I'm going to be sick."

Silence.

"I'm sorry, but I think I'm about to throw up." It was the truth. Surely the woman would understand that.

A raspy voice came from the stall.

"Sink's got a hole in it."

Kerry gaped at the stall door.

"Excuse me?"

"Sink's got a hole in it. You deaf?"

The woman sounded like a black grandmother. The accent was uncultured, maybe Alabama or south Georgia. Kerry considered a response that the woman wouldn't like, but thought better of it. The urge to vomit was powerful, the result imminent. She sighed with calculated exaggeration, and advanced to the sink in time to give in to the rising tide, which consisted first of fluid reminiscent of the morning's orange juice, followed by several violent dry heaves. Gasping, she turned on the water to drain her deposit, washing her hands thoroughly with soap from a dirty Dial dispenser. She reached for the paper-towel holder to the right of the sink. It was empty. She turned and scanned the back wall. No air dryer either.

Shaking her hands over the sink, she felt a sudden rage at the woman in the stall. Surely the old lady had heard Kerry in her misery, and yet sat there unconcerned. *Jesus. What a freaking selfish—*

"You with chile, honey?" The voice was softer than before, almost friendly.

What did she just say?

Kerry stopped shaking droplets off her hands.

"Excuse me?"

"You heard me, honey."

"Pardon me, but I am not your honey and I am definitely not with *child*. I was out late last night with some friends. Too many beers." Kerry finished drying her hands by wiping them back and forth on her khaki shorts.

"Beer ain't got nothin' to do with it, chile. You pregnant. You take good care uh dat baby now. Dat begins right now. Don't be drinkin' no more beers."

Kerry stepped to the stall door and placed her right palm against it. "I am not pregnant, and you can mind your own business. I am not your daughter. Mind your goddamn business."

"Chile, best you not be usin' words like dat. God's name in vain. Who been raisin' you?"

"Not you, whoever you are. Don't you have some pickaninny grandchildren to worry about?"

"Chile, diss is the third decade of the twenty-fust century. White women ain't supposed to call children pickaninnies no mo. You must be related to ol' Jeff Davis."

Kerry was appalled. Rage welled in her gut, then subsided. The old woman was just trying to get her goat. Probably sat in this stall all day to mess with women who were productively on their way to somewhere much better. Unlike the old woman. But no matter; Kerry would take the high road.

"Look, ma'am. I am not pregnant and I am *not* racist. Sorry about the word choice. You're just getting on my nerves. I hope you're proud of yourself. Goodbye."

Kerry pulled open the bathroom door just as the toilet was being flushed. The sound of the rushing water was like a sonic boom, surprising her in its power and then in its duration. Suddenly she wanted to be far away from the bathroom, this restaurant, this exit, this part of Tennessee. She did not want to see this woman emerge from the bathroom, and especially did not want this woman to see *her*. When she reached the restaurant exit, she paced impatiently as a white family of five entered single file, the father holding the door open for his wife, his three laughing kids, and then for Kerry, who thanked him under her breath and ran to her Volvo. She buckled up, started the ignition, set the satellite channel to the Beatles station, backed the vehicle out of its space, and stepped on the gas, not looking toward the restaurant lest she make eye contact with the black woman and give herself away.

Worry began to tug at her. Why did the woman so rudely speculate about Kerry being 'with chile'? She'd said it as if it weren't speculation. And that nonsense about Kerry using her mother's term for cute black children. Mom had always meant it as a compliment. Kerry had simply used the word in a moment of anger, with a woman she would never see face to face, so of course she didn't need to worry about it. But still… the woman had gotten to her, as if… well… as if she actually knew something.

That was ridiculous, naturally. Kerry set the cruise control at eighty-one after merging onto I-40. It was just an encounter with an old woman who had never been anywhere, whose favorite daily activity was sitting in a bathroom stall waiting for white women she could aggravate. For a moment, Kerry remembered Hattie, the family's black maid for the duration of Kerry's childhood. Hattie had doted on Kerry and her older brother, Erskine. But even as a kid Kerry had noticed conflict between Hattie and Kerry's mother. In retrospect, Hattie's comments about the family's comings and goings had been risky, like the time the family was packing for a trip to Hawaii. Hattie was cleaning the house, and soon would be watering the plants and managing the family's pets for a week in the Tisdales' absence. As Hattie helped Kerry's mother pack toiletries for the kids, Hattie said "Must be nice, goin' to Hawaii. Some day, lord. Some day."

Kerry's mother had stopped right then and replied, "It's called a vacation, Hattie. Erskine works very hard at his business, sometimes upwards of fifty hours a week. He deserves a trip like this from time to time."

To Kerry her mother's words had sounded like a rebuke. Kerry stopped working on the Disney crossword puzzle on the floor outside the master bathroom and did some math in her head. She knew her dad golfed on Saturdays and Sundays, usually with Mister Edwards and a couple of other friends from the club. On weekdays he liked his first martini at 5:30 sharp, with water crackers and extra-sharp cheddar cheese, which Hattie would set out every day before taking the bus home from the corner of West Paces Ferry and Dunlap. Dad enjoyed Mom's poached eggs before going to work every day, and those eggs were always on the plate at eight, before Mom took Kerry and Erskine to school. So her mother's response to Hattie resulted in Kerry's employment of the math. Her father's 45 hours away at the office each week were about the same as Hattie's hours splitting time between the Tisdales' home and the Edwardses' three houses down. Ever so briefly, Kerry had thought that maybe her mother was out of line. Hattie wanted to go to Hawaii someday, and Mom's response had suggested that such a thought was either ridiculous or inappropriate or both. Either that or Mom's response meant that she thought Hattie was trying to make her feel guilty. Kerry had felt the awkwardness of the silence that followed the rebuke. That silence had lasted for the next hour or so, interrupted only by the occasional "Ma'am, do you want Erskine's boat shoes to go on the trip?" or "How many flip flops does Kerry like to bring?" Mom's answers were terse on such days. And yet Hattie more and more frequently made comments that Kerry's mother didn't like.

Sometimes Hattie's comments were actually questions, but came off like comments. For example, there was the day the straw broke the camel's back. It was mid-summer. Kerry was sitting at the kitchen table eating a PBJ and doing her eighth-grade summer reading of Elie Weisel's *Night*, while Hattie was emptying the dishwasher and Mom was catching up on the *Parade* magazine from the previous Sunday. Hattie's question, as she settled a plate onto a stack in the glass-front cupboard to the right of the sink: "Kerry, where's that fancy private school sending you to college some day?"

Before Kerry could answer the question, her mother snapped the magazine shut. "Hattie, I am tired of you taking shots at our lifestyle and how we are raising our children. If you could afford it, you would do the same thing."

Then came Hattie's mistake, in which she was clearly out of line.

"Ma'am, if you and Miz Edwards paid me more, I could afford it. And my Thomas could go to school with your Kerry and Erskine, and Thomas wouldn't have to mow no more lawns when he could be doin' more homework to get ready for not cleanin' other people's houses when he's forty-six."

Kerry had squeezed her eyes shut. And then came her mother.

"You're done, Hattie. That's it. Get your things and leave. I will mail you your final check."

"Ma'am, I didn't mean nothin' by that. Maybe you and Miz Edwards can't afford more than the ten bucks an hour. I can appreciate that. Didn't mean nothin' by it. I do need my job. I'm very—"

"I said, get out now!" Kerry's mother had stood, flipping the magazine to the floor. "Every year, you get more and more bold, Hattie. Your job was to clean and help out around the house. If you didn't like the pay, you shouldn't have taken the job. Here or at the Edwardses, who are fine people and just as generous as we are. Now go."

Kerry had watched Hattie leave in silence, retrieving her purse from the granite countertop next to the refrigerator. Kerry examined her book, as if a spider were crawling across the front cover. She didn't lift her gaze until she heard the clap-clap of the kitchen screen door shutting behind the departed Hattie, who had always been instructed to use the kitchen door in coming and going. Kerry hadn't liked her mother in that moment, but this was her mother and this was Buckhead, not Lithonia, to which the bus would take sweet Hattie. Hattie had been unwise, Kerry knew. Now, en route to Memphis and her corporate future, Kerry remembered what her father had said when he learned at the dinner table what happened with Hattie: "Kerry? Erskine? Look at me. You learn something from this. Never disagree with the person who signs your paycheck. The world works just like your allowance. Now eat your asparagus if you have designs on dessert."

Kerry and her little brother ate their asparagus and drank all their milk.

As I-40 continued to flatten into the westward horizon, Kerry avoided the nagging, gnawing question. Was she with child, like the nasty old woman said from a graffiti-marred stall? If she was, Khalid was somewhere in Paris, the father of her first child now generously pleasuring another innocent American college graduate celebrating Phi Beta Kappa and hooking herself on café crème. She considered his obvious selfishness, his meaningless art, his self-obsessed passion for all things unpragmatic. He would never leave that life for the responsibilities of fatherhood. Never. She was certain of it. The bastard couldn't be bothered with protection. So why would he bother with raising a child? What a mother-f—

Her cell phone bleated on the center console. Kerry turned down the radio and looked at the phone. It said 'Unknown Caller.' She picked up the phone and answered, putting it into speaker mode. "Hello?"

"Honey, you need to take care a dat chile."

Kerry hit the brakes, swerving onto the right shoulder before correcting the Volvo back onto the road. She said nothing as her heart pounded.

"I know you can hear me, honey. See a doctor and call dat chile's daddy. Call your folks too, now. You got to take responsibility. Your life doan belong to you no mo."

She was imagining this. Had to be. That old woman was

still at McDonald's, and probably didn't even own a cell phone. Kerry was panicking was all, imagining this call the way she had imagined conversations with Hattie over the years. She pressed 'End' and refocused on the road.

It was the kind of thing Hattie would have said. Not to Kerry or Erskine, but to their mother. It just wasn't wise. What if Kerry turned around, headed east back to the McDonald's, spoke to the manager, charged the old woman with harassing a customer? The old woman was lucky that Kerry had to be in Memphis well before five o'clock.

Kerry changed the channel to First Wave, which was playing Billy Idol's "Eyes Without a Face." She tried to sing along:

"Eyes without a face... you got no human grace... you're eyes without a face... such a human waste... you're eyes with —"

The phone rang again. Kerry let the song continue. Surely the old woman wouldn't like Billy Idol. She answered and hit Speaker.

"How did you get my number?"

"Turn the music down, chile. You need to concentrate on dat road."

"How did you get my freaking *number*, you —"

"It was on the stall, chile. Right there on the stall. You put it there, remember?"

The old woman was insane.

"Why would I put it there, you old biddy? You are *crazy!* Leave me *alone!*"

"You know why you put it there, my darlin' chile."

Kerry pressed the brake when she realized she was about to pass a state trooper. She settled the Volvo into the right lane behind the cruiser.

"Darling *child?* I don't even know what you look like. Why are you harassing me? I don't deserve this. I'm just trying to get to Memphis to start my new job."

"I ain't harassin' you, chile. I'm helpin' you."

Kerry allowed silence to be her answer.

"Chile?" came the voice, sounding more and more familiar. "You know zactly why you put your number on that stall. You even put your name there for me."

This was ridiculous, Kerry knew. Maybe it was part of being sick. Delusions. Had she gotten enough sleep? Had someone slipped something into one of her beers last night in Buckhead? Either way, she knew she hadn't written her phone number on any effing bathroom stalls at that pit of an exit back there somewhere.

"Okay, old biddy. So tell me. Why would I do that, after you wouldn't even let me use the toilet to throw up? Why? Why would I *do that?*"

Silence again, this time chosen by the old black woman. Kerry pictured her, an old fat woman with an Aunt Jemima bandana in her hair. And then the old woman whispered something. Kerry barely heard it, the words somehow traveling audibly through Billy Idol's last descending notes.

"Because you want a real mother. Don't you, chile?"

Kerry stared ahead at the rear of the trooper's cruiser.

"I have a real mother," she said.

"You've come to me, chile. I can be your real mama. What say?"

"I'd say I have a future that starts at five o'clock in Memphis. Go away and leave me alone."

Kerry listened. She turned down a song by the Clash. There wasn't a thing about today that had anything to do with rocking a casbah. Maybe there never would be again. She pictured Khalid. He was older now, nursing a café crème. He was seated at a café table, a small child on his knee eating an ice cream cone. It looked like chocolate. A woman, maybe the child's mother, sat with her back to Kerry, oblivious to Kerry's long-

ing to be in that picture, in that café chair, sipping her own café
crème, soothing the child's younger sibling in her lap. An ache
grew in Kerry's throat as the Volvo drifted closer to the rear of
the state trooper's cruiser.

"Chile, your future ain't in Memphis. Not *dis* way. Cin-
cinnati neither. Your future's where you's honest and happy.
Come home to see me, chile. Jes' for a while. Come home and
see your mama."

Tears welled in Kerry's eyes, blurring her focus on the police car in front of her. She tapped the brake, falling back.

"I did give you my number. Didn't I, Hattie?"

Kerry held her breath. There was only one answer she wanted.

"Why, yes chile. Course you did. I'm your mama. Turn
around, sweet baby. Come home to me. After we get you some
rest, and some pie, and maybe do a Disney crossword puzzle,
how 'bout you call that fine young man? Give him the fabulous
news. He's got a gorgeous little girl comin' into dis world. And
dat little girl's goan have a darlin' great mama."

Kerry pulled the Volvo onto the shoulder and stopped. She
wiped her eyes with the backs of both hands.

"Will you teach me, Mama?" For the second time, she held
her breath.

"I already done did, chile. Just promise me dis one thing."

Kerry smiled, tasting salt at the corners of her mouth.
"What's that, Mama?"

"When you and that lovely man a yours take that chile
to Hawaii…"

"Don't you even finish that thought, Mama."

Silence.

"Mama?"

"Yes, chile."

"That was going to be *my* idea," Kerry said, pressing the
gas to re-enter traffic and reverse her direction at the exit up

ahead. The bridge over the highway looked new, and so did the McDonald's. After all, she was starting to feel sick again, gloriously sick, already tasting the thick chocolate milkshake that would carry her east toward all her tomorrows.

SECUNDO

I bet you know all about what goes on out there. Don't you, Rocket? Mom and Dad don't. Neither does Mills. She just thinks she does, especially about me. Are big sisters always like that? Sorry. How would you know? You don't have a big sister. But you understand me, don't you, Rocket? You might even be just like me. You've got secrets to tell, but you can't share them. Just like me. Not with people anyway. So tell you what. I'm going to give you a rawhide. The basted kind. You can listen and eat, since you probably already know this story. It's my secret. I think I know it now.

I was seven the first time I saved Roger Hudson's life. I was playing with Woody and Buzz, and Buzz says "Hey Dalton, look outside." So I look outside and I see a van in front of Roger's house. The van is white. A man in dirty grey overalls and a red baseball hat with curly black hair coming out that hole above where you latch the hat to make it looser or tighter gets out of the van and looks around, like he wants to be sure he's at the right house or something, or maybe he just wants to make sure nobody's looking. He walks to the back of his van and opens the back doors. They open sideways from the middle. He gets out this big grey toolbox and goes around the other side where I can't see him through our living room window, but in a couple seconds I see him again when he goes up the walk to Roger's front door. He rings the doorbell and looks around again. I move my head down when he does that, because I don't like what he's looking around for.

The front door opens. It's Mrs. Hudson. Roger's mom. You know. The pretty lady who brought you hot dogs after cook-outs. I know you're glad the Hudsons didn't have a dog. They didn't have rawhides either because they didn't have a dog, but they sure liked hot dogs, and they sure liked you.

So Roger's mom says something to the man in the white overalls and red hat. He looks around again, then says something to her. Mrs. Hudson pushes the man and tries to close the door. He pushes the door back into Mrs. Hudson and she falls down, so I don't see her anymore. The man looks around again before he goes in the door. For a second I thought he saw me in the window. So now the man is in the house even though that's the only place he wasn't looking until Mrs. Hudson opened the door. Well, I have to tell you. I was scared. Mrs. Hudson didn't seem to like that man. And he didn't seem to like her.

Mom was upstairs doing the laundry and watching one of her shows, I think the one she always recorded on the DVR about those doctors and nurses that solve murder mysteries and such. Mom would say no if I asked if I could go over to Roger's house on a Saturday when Dad and Roger's dad were playing golf and Mills was at her sleepover at Claudia's house and Mrs. Hudson was catching up on her shows that she was always telling Mom about but Mom never had time to try out. So I went out the front door as quiet as I could.

When I got across the street and went to the Hudsons' front door, I almost rang the doorbell. But that didn't seem like the smart thing to do, right? So I tried pushing down on the latch. It was locked. I guess the man in the overalls and the red hat locked it. That didn't seem good. So I walked around the left side of the house. When I got to the screen porch I tried the door. It was open. So was the big sliding door that went into the Hudsons' dining room. So I went in.

It was quiet. Roger was probably down in the rec room with his trains. I didn't hear anything yet, so I went down the hallway that went to the stairs that went down to their rec room. I got almost to the bottom of the stairs and stopped. The man in the overalls and red hat was standing there watching Roger. Roger was sitting on the carpet next to Thomas the train engine and Thomas's friends. Roger's eyes were really wide looking up at the man. Roger didn't see me yet. Neither did the man. I was a few steps from the bottom, being super quiet. Poor Mrs. Hudson was on the floor. She looked like she was asleep. Except there was some blood coming out of her nose. I think she hit her face on something. Or maybe the man did it. I don't know. I mean, I know now, but I didn't know then.

I backed up. Something bad was going to happen. I had to hide. So I crawled up the stairs and went back outside. I ran back across the street to my house to tell Mom what was happening. I got into the living room. When I was about to call Mom, Buzz said, "Dalton, go back out there. Get in the man's van and hide. You have to help Roger. Right now." I looked at Buzz like he was crazy. But Buzz was always right. So I went back out, but I was scared. I admit that to you. Really scared.

The van's back doors were still open like I said, so I got in. It was gross. It smelled like a dead rat or something, like the first cold day in the fall when Dad would turn on the heat and say "Crap, another rat died in the ductwork" because it smelled like a rat died in the ductwork and was getting cooked or something. Anyways, there was a big cardboard box behind the driver seat so I looked inside it and it was empty. I got in the box and pulled the four cardboard lids down over me as far as I could. Just in time too. I heard the man say "Shut up and get in" and then I heard a thump a few feet away from me toward the back. The doors slammed shut, but not together, like two claps a second apart when a teacher asks for our attention. But nobody had to ask for my attention. All of a sudden I had to go to the bathroom. Oh *God*. What was I going to do if I had to go to the *bathroom?*

I heard sniffling. Roger was crying, with a long high hum coming between the sniffles. The hum was coming from Roger's vocal chords. Then the doors opened again and I heard a crash. It must have been the toolbox. Then the doors slammed shut again, this time at exactly the same time, loud and hard like something final.

I started to cry too. I missed my mom and dad, even though Dad just left thirty minutes ago for golf with Roger's dad, and Mom was upstairs with her show and the laundry. I even missed Mills. But at least I was with my best friend, even though my best friend didn't know that yet.

I stopped crying when the driver door opened and I heard the rustle of the man in the overalls and red hat getting in. The door slammed, just as final as the back doors did. The engine started and I felt us moving. I closed my eyes and squeezed them tight. Music came on. I was surprised. I mean, not surprised that there was music. Dad loves playing music in the car. I was surprised that the man was singing along with it. It was a Frank Sinatra song that my dad liked a lot, something about this town being a lonesome town, an abuse you town, something like that about this town.

I didn't think a man who pushed Mrs. Hudson down and put Roger in this van would be like my dad in any way. I was surprised.

Maybe he wouldn't be concentrating while singing about an abuse you town. The box I was in was right behind the driver. I decided to risk poking my head out to see Roger. I folded out one of the cardboard flaps and peeked, right when the man was belting it out with Dad's friend Frank.

Roger was curled up in a ball in the middle of the floor, a couple of feet from the back doors. His hands and ankles were held together by wide silver tape. I think my dad had some. Duct tape, though my dad never used it for ducts. Maybe because of the dead rats that would get cooked in the ductwork when it got cold in the fall. The man in the overalls and red hat didn't seem to use it for ductwork either. I wondered whether he had ever used duct tape on a kid before now. When I decided that he had, I began to cry again.

I think Roger saw me crying out of the corner of his eye. He turned his head away from the back and toward me. There was silver tape covering his mouth. His eyes got really wide again, like in the rec room when he was looking up at the man who beat up his mom. But then his eyes looked glad. He had his best friend for company. So did I. I smiled at him. I don't really know why. We were in big trouble. The man in the overalls and red hat wasn't dressed like a clown, but I had read lots of news stories and stuff about men just like the man in the overalls. They didn't do nice things to kids. And sometimes they had white vans.

We had to get away from the man.

I wished I had Buzz with me. He would have told me what to do. I tried to imagine what Buzz would say, but he already said it. He said to get in the van. Help Roger and get in the van. He didn't say what to do next. This might be one of those times when Buzz said I had to use my imagination. I always got mad at Buzz for saying things like that. It's not as easy as being told what to do.

Right then my imagination wasn't being my friend. My imagination was showing me a dark place. A cold dark place that was damp and had rats. Not dead ones in my dad's ductwork either, but living squeaking ones in a cold dark place with music that was really nice on my dad's stereo, but really bad in the cold dark place. My imagination made me hear children crying in the cold dark place. How many children? Is the cold dark place where kids go when they die? Or is it a place where we go to find out how to use our imaginations?

I didn't want to go to this man's cold dark place, and for some reason I really, really, *really* didn't want Roger to go there. Like, I was more scared of Roger going there than of me going there. And I'm here to tell you, I did *not* want to go there.

Suddenly my box slid toward the middle when the van went around a turn. I dropped my head in case the man could see the box now. *Did he see me?* I swore a little, just in my head. My dad once said, when I got in trouble for using bad language in school, "Dalton, when you're about to swear, take a second first, and then swear in your head." It works. I swore in my head. I could even see the word in my head. It was the 's' word, the one I'd heard my dad say that one time in the garage when he hit his thumb with his hammer. In my head it was in italics. With a great big exclamation mark to go with it. It was the right word in my head when my box slid to the middle where the man could see it. But I didn't swear out loud. My dad said there's never much good in saying a cuss word out loud, especially when you're hiding in a box in a maybe-serial-killer's van.

The man didn't see me. He would've turned down the volume on Frank Sinatra. Now the song was "It Was a Really Good Year" or "very good year" or something like that. I remember like it was yesterday. Funny that I'm eighteen years old now and I have five of Dad's old Frank Sinatra albums in my music collection. I don't think a lot of people my age listen to Frank Sinatra, but Frank and Roger and I had a real adventure together.

So we made another turn and my box slid back over behind the driver again. This time he turned down the music. I held my breath. I looked at Roger, who was staring at me with eyes real wide like that guy named Tape Face in America's Got Talent a long time ago. I signaled with my hands and eyes for him to look somewhere else, but between the moving box and Roger staring at me, it was too late. The van slowed down. And then it stopped.

I could still hear Frank Sinatra, but his voice was faint. The words were "But now the days grow short… I'm in the autumn of the year…" and then the music was turned down all the way.

"Hey kid. Ya breathin' back there?" The voice was almost a whisper, all hoarse and raspy. Of course, Roger couldn't answer because right now Roger was like Tape Face, only for real in trouble, not trying to win a million dollars on a TV show.

Then I heard the sound of a garage door going up or down. I didn't know which, so I took a tiny peek and saw the right side of a white garage door finishing going up. The van moved again, and suddenly was real loud because we were in the dark garage and the door was going down behind us. Now my eyes were wide too, and I didn't even have tape over my mouth.

We were at his *house*. There was some light in the garage, even though the big garage door didn't have any windows. There must be a window somewhere. Maybe that was good, I thought. Maybe we could get away through a window. Unless he would put us in a basement or something. Suddenly I hoped that if we were in a basement or something and it was dark and cold and scary, maybe the man in the overalls and the red hat would play Frank Sinatra. Then I could pretend my dad was there and everything would be all right. But something told me that would be a really big pretend. Gi-normous.

The man opened his driver door. I pulled the flaps back over me and curled back up in the box. The man slammed the door. I could only listen now. It was quiet. Did he go inside the house?

The back doors of the van suddenly squeaked open, like the hinges were rusty. My dad would've put his WD-40 on them.

Maybe while listening to Frank Sinatra. *Dad!* But Dad was playing golf with Roger's dad. It was Saturday and that's what Dad did on Saturdays.

Then a raspy voice made me really, really cold.

"Boy, yer gonna be here a real long time," says the raspy voice. "Ya play nice, mind ya. Play nice and it won't all hurt so bad."

I heard the sound of sliding. It must've been Roger getting pulled to the open back doors. Then I heard a humming sound, but not like humming a song. It was Roger. Crying with tape over his mouth sounded like humming.

And then the humming got real frantic. High pitched. I think that was when Roger was being carried away, because then the humming got fainter kind of fast. When I heard another door slam, it wasn't the back doors of the van. It was a door to something else.

It was a door to inside.

I waited about a minute, and then opened the box flaps and sat up straight. The back doors of the van were still open, on account of the man carrying Roger into the house. I had to think fast, because what if he came back to close the van doors because the lights inside the van might be wasting the battery.

I knew I was too small to go inside and save Roger. I mean, I was only seven, so... but to get out of the garage and run for help, I would need to open the garage door. That would be real loud though, and the man in the overalls and red hat would run me down pretty quick. I climbed out the back and stepped down onto the concrete floor and almost didn't see the picture lying there. It must've fallen out of the man's overall pocket or something, because it wasn't dirty and it was folded in half. I spread it out flat in my hands.

It was a picture of Roger Hudson, who was inside the house right now. I didn't understand why the man would have a picture of Roger with him, but I didn't think the reason would be good. So I decided I better hurry. I shoved the picture into my right pants pocket and looked for the best way out.

I had to hurry *and* find the best way out *and* be quiet all at the same time. I found the window that was letting Saturday into the garage. The problem was that lots of rakes and hatchets and chainsaws and shovels were in a big pile in front of the window. I tried to reach over the pile but it was as high as my stomach and real thick. I couldn't touch the window. And there were nails in the sides and bottom of the window. The man must not've wanted people to get in the garage. Or get out either.

I turned toward the grey metal door that went into the house. My heart started to beat real fast, and I can tell you it already had a head start. I had to go in there. Suddenly I wondered if Dad was playing nine holes or eighteen. He and Mister Hudson wouldn't like knowing what Roger and I were doing right now.

Maybe Mom's show ended and she called downstairs to make sure I was okay, and then when I didn't answer she came downstairs and couldn't find me and got worried and called the Hudsons' house and got no answer and went over there and found Mrs. Hudson with blood drying on her face and woke up Mrs. Hudson and Mrs. Hudson told her what happened and Mom called Dad and Dad called the police and the police called the FBI and the police and FBI and maybe even the Army would arrive any minute proving they could find anyone who was in trouble.

Or maybe Mom's show had another ten minutes to go.

I had to go in there. Roger was in big trouble.

The door had strange carvings on it. Someone had taken a jack knife and made a symbol in bright red, red like the man's hat. The color really stood out because the door was grey. The symbol looked kind of like an animal's face, but also kind of like a person's face. The mouth was open, with fangs and everything, sort of like a wolf, but the nose was short like a person's, and the eyes… the eyes… the eyes were really mean. Like… evil. They were a person's eyes, and they were evil, the eyeballs black with white pupils—I didn't know they were called pupils then, but that's what was white, the pupils. And whoever painted the face made the eyes look like they could actually see me. Not just see me, but see my eyes and what was behind my eyes. The black eyes with the white pupils could see that I was more scared than I'd ever been in my whole life. They could see that I wanted to run away.

But they could also see that I wanted to help Roger. And that's when the eyes didn't just seem evil. They seemed angry all of a sudden. How could they do that? How could they change?

I put my hand on the door handle. It was cold. I squeezed it. And then I looked at the eyes again. They had changed. This time they weren't angry. They wanted me to come in, as if this was suddenly good news for the eyes… or good news for the fangs. That thought made me want to turn and run again. But Roger was my friend. He was my best friend.

I turned the handle and opened the door, very slowly at first. I was glad it didn't creak like in the movies. I swung the door open wide and went in.

The smell made me want to throw up. But I held it in, maybe because all I had for breakfast was a bowl of Apple Jacks. So I was able to stay quiet.

I was in a big kitchen. The windows weren't letting much light in because the shades were closed, so it was gloomy to go along with the smell, which my mom would sometimes say "was like something died." Well. I knew something died there. Or more than one something died. And then the something that died didn't get thrown away.

I tiptoed to the long kitchen counter that had the sink in it. There were lots of pictures on the counter, which had dirty yellow tile squares and lots of dirty plates with flies flying around them and landing and taking off again. The pictures were in black frames, lined up like they were going out to the playground for recess. I counted nine of them. I don't know why I counted them. It's not like it mattered how many there were... until I saw the first picture.

The boy in the picture was about my age. Maybe eight or nine. He had blond hair and wore a Pittsburgh Steelers tee shirt that was ripped at the neck by his left shoulder. He was crying when the picture was taken. His face was dirty, with a red smear on his right cheek. I just remember hoping it was red from a magic marker. But then I saw the rest of the pictures.

Some of the pictures were of boys, and some were girls. Just one kid in every picture, and now I noticed that they were all sitting in the same spot. Not together, not at the same time, but sitting in the same spot, on the floor next to a metal table that looked like it might be the kind you fold up when you're done with it. Like a table for playing cards or Monopoly or something like that. The floor in the pictures was concrete and had lots of dirt and white dust or something on it. I looked around me. The floor here in the kitchen had those square tiles that have patterns on them and look like whatever the sixties might have looked like. Not that I knew that then. But now that I've been in lots more houses, I know the difference between the new ones and the old ones. This house was an old one. A new one might have been just as bad because the man and the pictures were in it, but I could have pretended that people like my family lived there and liked to watch 'Finding Nemo' and 'Up' and drink chocolate milk and play 'Apples to Apples' and they didn't really put pictures of crying kids who missed their moms and dads on the kitchen counter, lined up like they were going somewhere worse than whatever was making them cry.

I looked at the picture of Roger that I held in my right hand. It had creases in it, the kind that make it look old. Roger was standing in front of the cereal section at the Publix near our neighborhood. He was holding a box of Captain Crunch. His mom was standing next to him, her left hand on the shopping cart and her right hand pulling down a big box of Total. Knowing Roger, he wanted the Captain Crunch. Knowing Roger's mom, she wanted the Total. Roger probably didn't win this argument, if they were arguing.

They didn't look like they knew somebody was taking their picture. I think it was the man in the overalls and the red hat. And now I had the picture and I didn't know where Roger and the man went. So I went through an opening that left the kitchen and went down a hallway. I stopped when I saw that there were more pictures, lots of them, hanging from the walls on both sides. I hoped they were pictures of the man and his family, and thought 'Please let them be pictures of the man and his family.' Maybe all dressed up for church. Or sitting on a blanket by Lake Franklin eating fried chicken from the Colonel and drinking cokes and laughing as if one of them just cut the cheese or something. But then the first picture made me want to throw up again. It was… it was…

I can't tell you about the kid in the picture, or any of the kids in the other pictures on the walls in that hallway. On account of I needed to find Roger, so I don't really remember. I just know that the kids in the kitchen pictures were right to cry. They were really right to cry. I wish they could have run away. But they couldn't. I know. Because the kids in the kitchen were also the kids in the hallway. And the kids in the hallway weren't kids anymore. And they never got to find out what it's like to be a grownup.

I wanted Roger to find out what it's like to be a grownup. So I reached the end of the hallway. There was a door on my left. It was painted black. Somehow I knew where it went. It went to the basement. The basement in my imagination. The cold and dark place was where Roger was.

I put my hand on the knob and turned it to the left. It wasn't locked. I pulled the door open, just a few inches.

It creaked. I said the 's' word in my head. If anyone was down in the basement in the cold and dark, they had to have heard the creak. I was frozen in place, looking through the opening. It was dark down there, like there weren't any windows. I listened, not sure what to do, whether to run, whether to keep opening the door, whether to yell out for Roger, yell out for help, whether to—

The raspy voice came from behind me.

"Are you sure you made the right choice, boy?"

I flung the door all the way open and ran down the stairs into the darkness. I almost tripped at the bottom when I missed the last step and landed on the concrete floor. I looked back up at the doorway. The man in the overalls stood in silhouette. He was laughing, a whispery laugh that sounded like he had a loud microphone but was just breathing into it. He wasn't coming down the stairs yet. I was frozen again. I would run if he started down the stairs, but I didn't want to run if that would *make* him come down the stairs. Know what I mean? He didn't move so neither did I. I wondered if he could hear my heartbeat pounding like a bongo drum. What if he's not coming down, just watching me, because Roger's not down here? The man could lock me in and go upstairs or wherever he had Roger and put Roger in pictures like the ones of those poor kids in the kitchen and on the hallway walls. I realized, looking up at the silhouette who was looking down at me and laughing like whispering, that now Roger was a poor kid too. And so was I.

The whispery laughter stopped.

"I know who you are, kid."

The man in the overalls had a voice that sounded like it was coming from right next to my ear. Like I had an earbud in my right ear and his voice was coming from inside the bud. It made me tingly all up and down the right side of my head and body.

The man spoke again. "I know who you *are*."

I couldn't say anything. My heart was beating really fast, and it made a sound in my ear. The sound was like someone using just the left side of a piano, over and over again, super fast. That's not what a heartbeat is supposed to sound like.

"Kid, I'm going to end your friend's life. There's no point in anybody ever finding out what he could have done as a grown-up. And you being who you are, you aren't going to want to watch. I promise you that. So… you will watch."

The man stepped down with his right foot. He was *coming*. His left foot joined his right. He stood on the first step and laughed again, the whisper of it close in my imaginary earbud. The tingle came back, all up and down my right side. I decided to say something. Maybe he would stop.

"You—you know who I am?"

I know I sounded scared, because my own voice came into the imaginary earbud, and the piano was playing right with it.

The man stood there on the first step. It was quiet. The piano slowed down, the same key playing over and over again, but not fast like before. I could tell that I had better pay attention. And then he spoke.

"You are here because of the boy." He stepped down onto the second step. "So am I."

His voice grew deeper with the last three words. I didn't know what to do. I took a step back, and looked to my right and left. On my right I saw what looked like a tricycle in the dark. There were also some kids' shoes, maybe six or seven. They were the Velcro kind, not the shoestring kind. That's all I could see in the darkness to my right. To my left I saw nothing at all, just a concrete floor and more darkness. Somewhere there must have been a furnace or something, or a water heater. Something like that. Maybe under the stairs. And I wasn't looking under there unless I had to.

The stairs creaked as the man took another step down toward me. I'm old enough now to say he "descended," because I've done pretty well in English class over the years, but right now I just remember every step *down*. I could feel his eyes on me, even though I couldn't see them.

I decided to say something again. Anything. He was taking his time, but that's because he knew he could. I needed to know how much time I really had. I gathered my breath and spoke.

"You said you know who I am."

The whispery laugh had some kind of whistle sound in it now. I wanted to wet my pants.

"Yes. I know who you are. I told you who you are."

"You—you did?"

"You are the one who helps this boy."

"Do you… know my name?"

The man took another step down.

"Yes."

"Wh-what is it?"

"You know your name."

"My name? My name is Dalton."

The whispery laugh whistled again. "Your name is Secundo."

***

It feels really weird to have someone say your name is something you've never heard of. Especially when the monster who says your name is Secundo has your best friend hidden

somewhere in a scary house and you're trapped in the basement and the monster who thinks your name is Secundo is getting ready to kill your best friend. And even more especially
when the monster who says your name is Secundo is laughing at you with this whispery whistly laugh that makes you
think that if this monster thinks your name is Secundo and not
Dalton, he must not actually be worried about it. I knew I was
named Dalton Evers, of course, but I also knew I wouldn't be
named *anything* much longer if I didn't think of a way to get
Roger and me out of there.

I began to wonder why the man in the overalls wasn't coming down—descending—faster. I was only seven and I wasn't
very big. And then I realized he was deciding something. He
was deciding about Roger. I had to keep him from turning
around and going back up there and locking the door.

"You're crazy. My name isn't Secundo."

"Nice try, kid. I'm going to leave you now. I have to end
your friend. I'll be back. Don't worry. You can watch the video."

"Where's Roger?" I asked.

The whispery laugh. "He's tied up at the moment. Enjoy
your stay. Your turn is in about an hour."

I looked for a light switch behind the man. There wasn't
one. The man laughed again, as if he knew what I was looking
for and the joke was on me.

"Ain't no lights down here, kid." The whistle came back
when he laughed again. Then he turned and clomped back up
the stairs, slamming the door and locking it with a really loud
click. Suddenly all I could see was a slit of light at the bottom
of the door.

I couldn't see. My eyes wouldn't adjust to the dark, like in
'Silence of the Lambs' when that FBI agent doesn't even know
the killer is right next to her. My eyes couldn't help me yet. So
I had to take Buzz's advice again. I had to use my imagination.

I imagined that the basement had more than just a tricycle and kids' toys and stuffed animals. What else would it have? Well... it would have a furnace somewhere, just like at our house and the Hudsons' house and all the other houses in our neighborhood. It would maybe have a hot water heater too. And a work bench with tools like my dad's. I imagined that if the furnace was like ours, it would have a flame that my dad called a pilot light. If I could find the furnace I could find the pilot light. If I could find the pilot light, I could feel around for something thin to light on fire by putting it through the hole to the flame that was the pilot light. If I could do that, I could use the something thin like a torch to see what else was down there. Not that I really wanted to see what else was down there in a child-killer's basement, but if I was going to save Roger I had to be able to see and I had to do it quick. The man might be hurting Roger. Like, right this minute.

I got on my hands and knees. Since I saw the tricycle and other stuff to the right of the stairs when the monster had the door open, I decided to crawl to my left where it looked empty. Maybe that was where the furnace was. Along the way I could feel around for something skinny that would burn.

After what I think was a few feet, my hands started to itch. The floor had some kind of flaky stuff on it. I rose up on my knees and rubbed my palms together, and that helped. I could feel flakes of something falling from my hands. I tried not to be disgusted by my imagination. My imagination was saying the flakes were old pieces of dead human skin. Dead children's skin. I almost threw up again, and boy again I was glad I only had Apple Jacks that morning. I thought of the pictures upstairs, the ones of kids on a concrete floor. This had to be the concrete floor. So were the flakes... no, I decided. My imagination needed to shut up for a few minutes.

And then I remembered the pictures, this time not because

my imagination was talking about flakes of dead children's skin getting stuck to my hands. This time I remembered them as I saw them. If this was the concrete floor, then it was also the floor under a table with a lamp on it. The lamp had a shade made out of leopard skin. The light in the pictures was coming from the leopard-skin lamp. If I could find the leopard-skin lamp, I could—

The door at the top of the stairs creaked open, just like it did when I tried to see what was down here when I was in the hallway. I froze there on my knees. Was he coming *down?*

I scrambled straight ahead into the dark, stopping when my right hand slid into something thin and hard. I resisted the idea that whatever it was must be disgusting or have something to do with death. I felt it with my fingers. It was made of wood. A table leg? I felt around with my left hand, and sure enough there was a second wooden post. I had found a table. I crawled between the two legs and reached further ahead into the dark. There was a cold flat surface. A wall. A concrete wall. I huddled against the wall, under a table that might or might not have a leopard-skin lamp on it, and waited.

The stairs began to creak as the man came down, descended, one step at a time. He was taking his time. And then he spoke.

"*Secundo…* I want you to see your *friend.*"

I still didn't understand the first word. It sounded like he was swearing. And then there was another creak. And another. I breathed as shallowly as I could, in case he could hear the fear in my breath.

"*Secundo!* Tell me where you are. Your friend is with me. Tell me where you are, secundo." The whispery laugh followed, but it didn't sound like he was trying to be funny. I stayed silent. How did I know whether Roger was really with him?

Another creak, as if he was being careful. But why was he being careful? I was only seven. So was Roger. And this man was *big.*

The silence started to get really loud. I was shaking from trying to breathe just a tiny bit at a time. And then came the explosion.

"SECUNDO! Speak or show yourself *NOW OR YOUR FRIEND DIES!"*

The man was angry with me. I was used to doing what grownups said, especially when they were mad at me, and the man in the overalls and red hat was really mad.

I decided to say something so he wouldn't kill Roger right then and there.

"My name is not Secundo." I surprised myself by saying it like I meant it. Of course I meant it, because the man wasn't making any sense. But still, I was surprised I said it louder than a whisper, what with how much shaking I was doing.

"Stay where you are, secundo. Mother says it's time to end you."

A creak. And another. And another. He wasn't taking his time anymore, which meant he was never being careful. He was just being quiet, listening for me. And now he knew where I was. I had to speak again before he made it all the way down the stairs.

"If Roger is with you, prove it."

The whispery laugh, then: "Okidoke."

I had never heard Roger scream, or anyone else except in the movies. The scream was very high-pitched. I felt my eardrums rattle. And then I heard Roger crying. No words. Just crying, with his voice being part of it every time he exhaled into his sobs. What did the monster do to him?

"Was that good enough for you, secundo?"

I hesitated. I should not be defiant, I thought.

"Yes," I said, in barely more than a whisper.

"I'm going to turn the light on now, secundo. Stay where you are. It sounds like you are right where I need you to be. My camera is on a fixed tripod, you see." The creaks resumed.

I didn't know what a tripod was when I was seven, but I knew that he meant I was right in the spot where he took those pictures hanging in the hallway upstairs. That made me feel really sick in my stomach. Once again I was glad I only had Apple Jacks for breakfast that morning.

Suddenly there was light, coming from a naked light bulb hanging from the middle of the ceiling. There wasn't another creak yet, so he must have wanted me to look around a little before making his arrival with Roger. My heart started pounding really hard and fast when I saw the rocking chair in the middle of the floor. Not because there was a rocking chair, but because of what was in it.

The little girl wore a dress that made me think of Little Orphan Annie. She had brown hair in pigtails, and on her feet were black saddle shoes that made me think of what kids looked like when my grandfather was a kid. Her eyes stared straight ahead, and her freckled face seemed stuck between smiling and crying. In her lap was a teddy bear, but not a brown one. It was a polar bear. The girl's left arm was around the polar bear as if she loved it. She probably did. Or used to.

The little girl was real, but very still. Nothing moved. Not even her eyes. And then I knew. The little girl who used to be real was stuffed. Like the big fish and deer heads and even a pheasant in the den with the old wood paneling at the Harrisons' house down the street.

I threw up my Apple Jacks. And then I threw up again, spitting when I was done.

He laughed a scary, raspy laugh, from what sounded like the bottom of the stairs. Any second now he would round the corner with Roger still crying. And my best friend and I would become pictures in the hallway. Maybe even stuffed and put in another rocking chair. I looked again at the little girl, and it occurred to me that maybe she had been in that rocking chair for fifty years. What if that was what she was wearing the day her mommy and daddy couldn't find her? What if the monster was immortal? Or his daddy and granddaddy were just like him?

What if the monster's daddy and granddaddy told him about "secundos"? What did he mean by that name?

"Before I grace your awed vision with my presence," the monster said from around the corner, "you must answer one question, secundo."

I was afraid to speak. He continued.

"Do you want to die before your friend dies? I will give you that courtesy, seeing as you are a secundo and might not want to watch your friend's slow death. After all, it is you that I most wanted today. Your friend was the lure. You are the catch. And in your failure as a secundo, your friend is the succulent gravy that makes your end so much more delicious."

I remained silent.

"You begin to anger me, secundo. Choose."

I don't know where the words came from. They just came, as if I heard them without saying them:

"I choose to go first."

"Good. Wise choice, Secundo."

Another creak, followed by the scrape of a shoe on concrete, revealed that the monster had actually been standing on the second-from-bottom step. And then he was there. Only now he wore something wildly different from his overalls and red hat. I wanted to run, to fly, to disappear, *anything* but see the monster in what he wore now.

His head was that of a large wolf. It was a stuffed real head, like the little girl's. The monster wore it like a Darth Vader helmet. The wolf's eyes were there, fixed in a vicious stare that seemed to see me. The real eye holes must have been in the wolf's fur somewhere, since part of the head was the thick furry neck.

His body was covered in tattoos, except for black pants that were too short, coming only halfway between his knees and his ankles, as if the pants were really someone else's, or as if he had worn these pants since the seventh grade.

The tattoos were all of children. Smiling, happy children. There were children on his bare feet. There were children on his ankles, and above his ankles until they disappeared under the black pants. There must have been children inside the black pants, out of the light.

His arms were covered with children, disappearing under the short sleeves of his tee shirt, which was a dark red. I wouldn't have said "crimson" when I was seven, but the tee shirt was crimson. The children came back out above the neckline of the tee shirt, just for a couple of inches before disappearing upward into the wolf head. I guess the overalls had high collars, because I didn't remember seeing tattoos when I saw the man in the overalls.

I don't know how long I stared at the monster. He was letting me stare, enjoying it for sure, and at some point I looked at my best friend. Roger was held up by his hair, the monster's left hand curled into the thick hair on the back of Roger's head. Through closed eyes squeezed shut, Roger continued to cry. Nobody in the universe could have blamed him.

And nobody in the universe could have blamed *me*. I wanted to cry, my despair was so great. But I didn't. As I told you, I threw up when I saw the little girl in the rocking chair, so I guess that was my turn already. And then the monster spoke.

"I see that you are impressed. In awe, even." The monster's voice was muffled a little bit by the wolf head, but I heard him clearly. "You like the children, secundo?"

I considered not answering, but I thought that would upset him, and now would not be the time to do that. So I answered. I was honest.

"No."

"No, secundo? Why? Because you weren't a secundo to them? It wouldn't have mattered. I collected them, one by one. You may have seen some of their pictures up in the hallway? The kitchen? Ah... I see that you have. Now I get to collect your friend. But don't worry. He will live on in the artwork of my epidermis."

I was seven. I didn't know what "epidermis" meant. And he knew it.

"My skin, secundo. Roger will live on as art on my skin. As photography in my hall and my kitchen. Maybe even as 3-D art in another rocking chair. A proud legacy."

I didn't know what "legacy" meant either. But that's what he said. I figured it out from what my English teacher in sixth grade later called "context." I figured out what "legacy" meant from "context," even though we hadn't learned either of those words in second grade. I guess I could have done the same thing with "epidermis." Maybe the monster knew I just didn't want to.

***

I knew the wolf's eyes were dead, but they zeroed in on my eyes anyway. They had some red in them. Some black too. And they were mean. I didn't understand why they would look mean toward me. I wasn't the one who made them dead, and I wasn't the one who made them look alive again. But they stared hard at me. Somehow the monster made them look like that.

Roger's eyes were still squeezed shut when he was set down on the floor next to the rocking chair with the little girl in it. He didn't have tape over his mouth anymore. I guess that's why I heard him scream so clearly. His legs and arms weren't tied up either. I think the monster knew Roger wasn't going anywhere without my help. And I think I knew the monster was right, because just as the monster was bending over and adjusting Roger to sit and watch my execution, I heard Buzz whisper "Now!" in my right ear, like he did sometimes when he wasn't in the same room as me.

I jumped to my feet and rushed into the backside of the monster with everything I had, which wasn't much when I was seven, but he was bending over and it was enough. He fell forward away from the rocker, past Roger and onto the concrete floor with a thudding sound. I didn't watch but I think the wolf head hit the floor because his forearm didn't first. I heard the monster curse as I grabbed Roger by the left arm and we ran, ran, *ran*—out of the room and up the stairs and through the door into the hallway. I slammed the door shut just as I heard the monster clomping up the stairs and screaming the f-bomb over and over again, mixed with something about killing the f-bomb out of that f-bombing secundo. I fumbled with the dead-bolt latch, which had been used maybe hundreds of times to lock future dead kids and future tattoos and future pictures and even future rocking-chair dolls in the basement. I shot the deadbolt all the way across just as the doorknob turned and rattled violently.

I looked at Roger, who was standing to my left and shaking. I held up my finger to shush him, but I think that was unnecessary, especially when the monster began pounding on the door and cursing, some in English and some in a language I didn't recognize. Maybe it was the language of whatever 'Secundo' was. It sure wasn't me.

I grabbed Roger's arm and pushed him in the direction of the kitchen. The pounding and cursing continued behind us, as Roger stopped to look at one of the hallway pictures closest to the kitchen opening. He pointed at the picture, which was of a boy, maybe six years old. That's all I want to tell you.

"That's Carolyn Simpson's brother," Roger whispered. "Remember when his picture went on those milk cartons everywhere? He was older than us in Sunday school."

I took a long look. Roger was right. It was Ricky Simpson. He would have been about eleven now. I shivered.

"We gotta go, Roger."

The cursing stopped for a moment, then resumed, but this time instead of the pounding there was a loud splintering sound. We froze and stared at the door. The splintering came again with a whack.

The monster had an axe.

"Run!" I yelled.

Roger was already on his way. I caught up with him halfway through the kitchen and directed him to the garage. There had to be a button for raising the garage door. I heard the splintering again, and now it was repeating faster. The door to the garage was already open as I had left it. I looked on the wall next to the doorway, and sure enough there was a panel of three buttons. I pushed the first one. The garage light came on above the white van.

Splinter!

I pushed the second button. My hand was shaking. Nothing happened with the second button.

Splinter!

The monster was almost through the door. I reached for the third button just as Roger said he'd peed his pants. I pushed it.

The garage door started going up. We rushed toward the rising opening and bent down to get underneath it because it was so slow. As we got outside we heard the monster again. His cursing was louder.

He was through the basement door.

"Don't look back, Roger!" I hissed as we ran for our lives, out the straight driveway and into the street. There were no cars coming. We had to keep running, so we turned left and sprinted. The cursing stopped. Maybe he gave up. As we ran I turned to look back.

The monster had not given up. He was maybe fifty feet behind us and gaining. He had stopped cursing because he was outside. He just wanted to catch us and bring us back without too much noise.

So *we* had to make the noise, right?

"HELP!" I screamed as loud as I could.

"HELP!" Roger screamed as loud as he could.

We ran and screamed for help. Ran and screamed for help. I looked back, hoping the screaming had made him quit so he wouldn't get caught.

Thirty feet, maybe. He wasn't quitting. And then he yelled something chilling.

"I'm going to kill your **MOTHERS** if you don't come **BACK!**"

I looked back again. I don't think he was used to running a lot, because now we were back up to forty feet. That must've been why he threatened our mothers. Either way, I was glad for two things: one, he wasn't used to running, and Roger and I were, since we played touch football most days after school and on weekends at Rockwood Park. Two, he didn't come after us in the white van. If he went back now to get it, we would be long gone. Three... oh yeah, there weren't three things I was glad for. But there was one thing I wasn't glad for. What if he went back for the white van and went straight to our houses and killed our moms before we could find our way home. We knew we weren't far from our street, but we didn't know where we were.

I turned to look again as we ran. The monster had the same idea I did. He was running back toward his house. If he were walking, that would mean he quit. But he was running, even though he was slow from being tired.

He was going back for the white van.

"Roger! Stop! He's going back. I think he's getting his van. We have to save our moms!"

Roger stopped, breathing heavily like me.

"Follow me," I said. We ran to the closest house, a two-story brick house on our right. I rang the front doorbell over and over again, figuring it would be harder for somebody watching a TV show to ignore the doorbell if I rang over and over again.

I was right. The door opened. The man in the doorway was about my dad's age, with some white hair sprinkled in with lots of black. He even reminded me of my dad a little bit. He had friendly eyes. He even looked like he was dressed for golf. Just like my dad.

"Gentlemen," he said with a smile. "Are you... okay?"

I gushed all at once.

"The monster with the white van is after us! He kidnapped Roger and was going to kill him and stuff him and take pictures of him and put a tattoo of him on his arm or something and we got away and he's gonna kill our *moms* now if we—"

"Whoa! Slow down, buddy, slow down. Just relax a second." The man looked up and down the street. "Where is this man now?"

"I think he went back to get his van and go kill our moms and please help us maybe call the police or take us home or—"

"Whoa again, young fella. Is that the van right there?" He pointed to his left.

I turned and looked. To my horror, the white van was coming in our direction and slowing down. Then it pulled over to the curb right in front of the house.

Roger screamed and ran past the man into the house. I almost did the same.

"Yes, that's him! Don't let him take us!" I grabbed the man's left hand. "Please!"

"Now, now, young fella. I'm sure this will all be fine. See? He's getting out now. I will take care of this." The man patted me on the head with his right hand.

The monster got out of the car. He was back in the overalls and the red hat. He strolled up the walk as if he had all day, smiling like he didn't have a care in the world. He got within ten feet and stopped.

"Hey Bob," said the monster in a voice I hadn't heard today. He sounded like he and Bob were friends.

"Hey Charlie," said the friendly man who dressed like my dad on Saturdays. "No jobs today?"

"Ha!" the monster replied. "I wish. Heading out for a ruptured water line over in Standish Mews." He laughed and looked at me. "Dalton, I promised your mom and dad I would keep you until three today. You know that. Now come along." I was speechless. The monster smiled at the friendly man again. "Bob, I think I've got to stop doing favors for friends. Or else get married and have kids of my own. Sometimes I feel like I have lots of them." He chuckled as if laughing at himself.

The friendly man shifted, still holding my hand.

"Charlie, these kids are terrified. They said you took one of them, and that you said you're going to kill their moms. What's going on here?"

The monster looked at me as if I were his favorite kid in the world.

"Dalton. I said your moms were going to kill *me* if I didn't keep you out of trouble. Kill *me*. Not me kill *them*. I was joking, Dalton. You love the drama, that's for sure! Ha ha!" He smiled again at the friendly man. "These boys have wild imaginations."

I had to speak up. The monster seemed so nice all of a sudden.

"You're a killer! You kill kids and stuff them and do tattoos of them. You even turn them into dolls. And you don't know our moms! Show Bob your arms!"

"Your arms?" Bob asked, curious. After all, he was in the middle of a very unusual Saturday now. "Charlie, this is very strange. What's this boy talking about?"

The monster laughed softly.

"Dalton's been like this ever since his uncle got killed in Afghanistan. The trauma, well… they were close. Very—"

"I don't *have* an uncle!" I screamed.

"Not anymore," said the monster. "Bob, that's the core of the problem. And now Dalton likes to talk about my tattoos. As if there's a law against body art. It's all a little sad."

Bob squeezed my hand and said, "Show me the tattoos, Charlie."

The monster stared at the friendly man. "This is silly, Bob. Just give me the kids. I promised their parents."

"Show me the tattoos, Charlie. Or I call the police."

My heart was beating so hard, I thought Bob and the monster could both hear it. Everything depended on the friendly man now. Everything. I looked behind me into the house.

Roger was gone. Or at least I couldn't see him. Maybe he'd found a phone and called the police. We both knew how to dial 911. Or maybe he'd gone out the back.

The monster broke the silence. "Okay, Bob. I will show you the tattoos. Inside, if that's okay. They're kind of private. That's why I don't wear tee shirts."

"Yes, you do!" I blurted. "And you wear a wolf's head when you kill children!"

The monster's eyes clouded. "Shut up, you little punk," he said, before realizing it and smiling again at Bob. "What an imagination! Ha!"

The friendly man sounded less friendly now. "Charlie, I need to see the tattoos right now. This is disturbing me, man. I don't know you that well. Come in and let's take a look."

"No!" I shouted. "Not inside!"

But it was too late. Bob walked me in and the monster followed. Once we were in the front hall, Bob closed the door.

"Here," he motioned to his left. "The living room." He ushered us in. I was careful to keep Bob between the monster and me.

"Where's Roger?" the monster asked.

"Probably hiding, from what this boy's been telling me. I hope he doesn't have a reason to be, Charlie. You know how I feel about this sort of thing." He paused. "Ricky's been gone for three years now. Disappeared right from our back yard."

Ricky? Oh my God, I thought.

The monster reached out and put his hand on the friendly man's shoulder. "The whole neighborhood continues to grieve with you, Bob."

Ricky?

"Sir?" I said.

Bob's eyes had welled up.

"Yes?"

"Are you Mister Simpson? Carolyn's dad?"

The friendly man looked down at me. He looked scared all of a sudden.

"Why, why yes. Do you know Carolyn?" I could see he might even hope I didn't.

"Yes, sir. This monster has her brother's picture in his house. From when he was little. Lots of other kids too. He—"

The monster was on the friendly man before I could say the next word. They tumbled onto the floor, the monster grabbing the friendly man's head and banging it over and over again against the hardwood. I tried to pull him off, but he was vicious, cursing again, this time about killing the f-word out of effing Bob. He was going to kill him. I should've run, but couldn't. I just kept pulling at him, and started hitting his head, but the monster didn't care and I was too small to save the friendly man. I looked up at the sound of Roger's voice. Roger stood in the front hall.

"They're on the way," Roger said. Then he said it again. The monster stopped, as if listening.

The sound of sirens interrupted from a distance. I jumped up and ran, pulling Roger with me and up the stairs, not knowing where we were going, but knowing that the monster couldn't follow us. His time was running out.

We stopped at the top of the stairs. The monster named Charlie stood at the bottom, the look in his eyes saying he might just come on up. But his wits got the better of him, and he turned and ran out the front door. The sirens grew louder. I said "Stay here." Roger didn't have a problem with that. I went down the stairs in time to see the white van pulling forward out into the street heading off to my right. I called up to Roger.

"Roger! Did you tell them about the white van?"

"Um. No. I don't even know where we are. They just said they were on the way."

My dad would've said to me, "Oh sweet baby Jesus. You should've told them about the white van." I just said to Roger, "Oh. Then they're not gonna catch him."

Roger came down the stairs. We looked at the friendly man. Bob's eyes were open. They stared at a single spot on the wood floor. The eyes didn't move. Neither did Bob. And then Roger and I started to cry. We cried for Bob. We cried for kids in pictures. We cried for our mothers. We cried for ourselves.

And when we were done with those reasons, we cried for the whole world, because we didn't know the answer to a very big question:

What happens if the best grownups are dead?

WEEDING FOR
EISENHOWER

✳ ✳ ✳

L ess than four months into Paul Garrett's tenure as head-master of Saxby Academy, Mrs. Mary George Sanders LeGrande Taskill was emphatic in her right-this-instant instruction to the new headmaster. "Charles is *not* to enter your office, Mr. Garrett. You had best understand that right *now*," said Mrs. Taskill, her voice mixing a nasal stoppage with an authoritative ring and a Lowcountry accent borne of generations of superior breeding and culture. "Charles is **NOT** going in there!"

Paul Garrett, holding the phone a couple of inches from his ear to compensate for the rising shrillness, examined the faded edge of his Duke University mousepad and pondered Mrs. Taskill's words. He wasn't sure what was most disturbing: her belief in the strategy of intimidation, or her conviction that her son was completely incapable of errors in judgment at the accomplished, wise, integrity-drenched age of thirteen.

Paul shook his head, smiled at the exhausted mousepad, and tried to convey the obviousness of his response.

"Mary George, let me be clear. Charles is absolutely coming into my office. All four boys are joining me, as soon as they arrive with Ms. Westridge. This is a critical part of their education, Mary George. A part of growing up well. Trading unkind insults on Facebook is unacceptable behavior. The conversation which is about to take place in my office will be an important one for you to support at the dinner table. I hope I can count on you and your husband for that supp—"

"*Spare me* that mission and philosophy crap, Mr. Garrett. Charles is *not* coming in there. Not with *that* boy who shouldn't be at the Academy in the first place! That's all there is to it. Charles is not going in. Do you understand me? I have told him not to go in, and he's not going in. Don't you *make* him!"

That might've been a hiss, Paul mused as the expected knock came at the door. Sandy Westridge, the grandmotherly head of the middle school at Saxby Academy, poked her head in. "They're here," she said. "But Charles insists that his mom told him on his cell phone that he doesn't have to come in. What should I do?"

Paul felt sorry for the terrified woman. Her head seemed wedged between door and jamb, her pale face framed by short greying hair, the cream of the jamb and the heavy oak door squeezing her head in the vise grip of the modern power of children to manipulate their parents.

"Bring them in, Sandy."

"Do you mean *all* of them?"

Paul spoke in answer, both to his employee and for the telephone ear of the mother of United States Senator William Le-Grande's nephew.

"Of course I mean all of them. None of these boys will be robbed of the teachable moment, Sandy. We don't under-educate, even when undereducation is requested by a parent."

Paul returned the phone to his ear. "*That* boy, as you refer to him, has as much right to be here as any other child, Mary George. Eric Horton is coming into my office with Charles and the other boys because **ALL** of these boys acted badly. They will be treated equally. The boys are here, Mary George. I've heard your request. We'll be in touch after—"

The eruption was instant.

"No! This is not a *request*, Mr. Garrett. I'm coming over there right now, and I'm bringing my lawyer. Charles is *not* going in there! He's **NOT**…"

Paul heard nothing more. He said "Have a nice afternoon" and hung up the phone.

He rose and approached the door to greet the four boys, all of whom the headmaster liked. They entered with sheepish expressions directed downward at the grey carpet. Trailing them was Sandy Westridge, who looked like she would benefit from a handful of Excedrin.

The headmaster shook the hand of each of the boys and told them to sit down. Two chose the dark leather sofa, while the others sought refuge in captain's chairs which bore the crest and name of Saxby Academy. The headmaster decided to regard them quietly, equally, for a few moments, allowing silence to press its weight onto the room.

Paul Garrett was a tall man, about six-foot-four, with thick brown hair sprinkled with grey. Since the beginning of his teaching career nineteen years earlier, Paul had been aware of and enjoyed the respect he received from children, whether he deserved it or not, even from the most immature or cynical of students. He never hesitated to take advantage of the opportunity such respect gave him when teachable moments arose, which were frequent if educators were paying attention, and to him were part and parcel of the education and growth of quality human beings.

As Paul let his gaze fall on four erring boys on this crisp October afternoon, he couldn't help but curse himself for resenting their parents with a fervor that he knew would not diminish in the coming months. Just four months into the job, and already he was appalled at their parents for treating teachers like indentured servants easily replaced at some professional trading post. He recoiled at their parents' assumption that tuition dollars purchased the right to attack, to disparage, to embarrass people who choose to teach children for a living. But most of all, Paul Garrett hated the knowledge that the conversation which he was about to have with these boys would be undone in at least two of these four households within minutes of the boys going home to their mothers. Two of the mothers, after all, were members of The Daffodil Society.

***

Franklin Redstone was the eldest of local real estate magnate and boat dealer Harold Redstone's three sons. A graduate of Saxby Academy, Franklin had recently been promoted by his father to the post of President of Redstone Marine. Franklin was very proud of this accomplishment. Often over lunch or a cold one at the 19th Hole he would quietly and modestly let companions know that forty-three is a young age for CEO's. As Saxby Academy's new chairman of the board of trustees, he felt further compelled to share that his education was the number one factor in his meteoric rise to the top of Redstone Marine, aside of course from his Protestant work ethic. His four children were lower-school students at Saxby Academy, and he was proud to see them following in his footsteps as an achiever.

Franklin had joined the board only a month ago, at the request of his friend, Senator Bill LeGrande, who had complained that the time the senator was spending in Washington was affecting his oversight of the Academy. The senator explained that he was stepping down from the board due to attendance requirements, and wanted a leading alumnus like Franklin to take his place, especially to keep an eye on the new headmaster, who already in some folks' minds was behaving as if it was *his* school. Franklin had agreed that folks who moved to Banfield from Atlanta, Chicago, Charlotte, New York and such places needed careful watching. Paul Garrett seemed like the poster child for intrusion on the Banfield way of life and the order of things. He was becoming too popular too quickly, and if families like the LeGrandes, Redstones, Taskills, and other leading and historic clans didn't come together to keep watch over the preservation of the order of things, the yankees and the Atlantans (same difference) would take over.

So when Jack Sculley had his heart attack three weeks ago, the senator sent an email to all the board members insisting that Franklin Redstone replace Jack as board chairman if Jack was unable to recuperate quickly from his quadruple heart bypass. After all, though Franklin was new to the board and to governance of independent schools, he was a graduate of the school and a leading business executive and therefore perfect for the role of chairman. Paul Garrett, the new headmaster, weighed in with his opinion that Jim Tankersley, the vice chair, should assume temporary leadership duties until Jack Sculley could resume the chairmanship. The headmaster's argument was that Jack and Jim had played a key role in bringing Paul to Banfield and the Academy, and that their partnership was close and effective, as evidenced by the sharp increase already in enrollment, gifts to the school, and the positive responses to the swift and broad changes the new headmaster had made since July 1st.

The senator's email prevailed. Jack Sculley was thanked profusely by the board for his service as chairman, received a beautiful Academy rocking chair engraved with his name and dates of service, and was prayed for fervently by everyone on the board for a full and complete recovery. Jim Tankersley resigned in response to the snub. Franklin Redstone recognized the awesome responsibilities which came with chairmanship, and so he sent a letter to all the school's families sharing the board's commitment to running the school in the tradition which had been established by the founders in 1965. In the letter he said "The buck stops here, so feel free to bring any complaints directly to me or to other leaders on the board. We are here for you!"

This Garrett fellow had responded to Franklin's letter with

two comments which Franklin felt were out of line, but he had decided that as a leader he would generously tolerate disagreement, just as he did with his boat salesmen at Redstone Marine. The headmaster's first comment had been to "remind" Franklin that the headmaster, not the board, is in charge of the day-to-day operations of the school, and that complaints, "all of them," should be directed to the educators at the school. Garrett's second comment had been that some of the traditions established in 1965 were reasons why the school had struggled so mightily in recent times. The headmaster obnoxiously went on to add a pile of drivel about some short story called "The Lottery" as meaning that we should "examine our traditions" to make sure they're worth keeping. Franklin had briefly considered finding the story somewhere and reading it, but decided instead, as a good one-minute manager, to ask his egghead cousin Hank if he knew the story. Hank said yeah, that he read it in eighth grade, and it was a stupid story about people in a town killing a citizen every year with a bunch of stones. Hank had made the honor roll every year at the Academy in the early 1980's, and he said he never heard any damned thing from the teacher about the story having something stupid to do with examining your traditions.

"Sounds like bullcrap to me," said Franklin.

"It's bullcrap," said Hank.

So Franklin avoided wasting his time on the stupid story. Instead, he saw that the headmaster was out of touch with Banfield, and resolved to keep the close watch that he had promised to the senator, to the senator's wife Tandy, and also to the community.

It was this resolve that brought Franklin Redstone to his meeting with the headmaster a full ten minutes early. He strolled casually past the receptionist's desk. She asked him to have a seat while she notified the headmaster that he was here, but Franklin saw that the headmaster's door was open, so he said he would go ahead and pop his head in. After all, at Redstone Marine if he said he would pop his head in, that meant he would pop his head in. There was no reason why it should be different at the Academy.

When he got to the door, he saw Paul Garrett typing at his desk overlooking the front entrance to the school. The board chairman rapped twice on the oak. The headmaster swiveled in his black leather chair.

"Franklin! Come on in and have a seat." The headmaster rose from his chair, glancing once more at the computer screen as he did so.

"Sorry I'm early, Paul," said Franklin Redstone as he sank into one of the captain's chairs arranged in a semicircle facing the leather sofa.

"Not a problem," said the headmaster, sitting down in a chair next to the book-lined wall.

"So…" said Franklin. "You got my email."

"I did. Both of them."

"So we're clear."

"About what?"

"About the records and the apology."

"No."

"No?"

"No."

"You mean I wasn't clear?"

"Your clarity was fine. But the boys are pulling weeds together as a productive consequence. There was never anything going into their records, Franklin. They met with me, we had a great conversation, and they're fine kids who needed a chance to learn something about how we don't treat other human beings. There will be no apology to Charles and his family, as there is none due. I hope this is clear, and I hope I have your support."

Franklin looked the headmaster in the eye, the way he did when one of his employees at Redstone Marine needed adjustment. The headmaster returned his gaze, annoying him with a stare that seemed a bit inappropriate to Franklin.

"Paul, you have no right to discipline these boys over something that happened at home. I expect you to drop this thing and tell Mary George and the kid that you're sorry. Any way you want, though. I want to help you out on that one. Any way you want. Letter, email, text, phone call, you name it. Fax, even."

"If I owed them an apology, Franklin, I would deliver it in person, and it would be genuine. But let me share this with you. You said, as Mary George did, that this happened at home. That misses the point educationally. This happened at night. The fact that the boys were using their computers or smartphones to bully, disparage or embarrass each other so cruelly is merely incidental. They are fellow citizens at this school and in the community, and they need to learn now, right now, that this behavior is not acceptable. I would be remiss as a teacher if I were to ignore this behavior and excuse it simply because these boys sent these profane and unkind messages from home rather than from or at school. Really, this is a time when support from the board is critical, Franklin. We don't know each other well yet, not like Jack Sculley and I do, but this is a prime example of when a board must back the headmaster."

"Let's get something straight, Paul," said Franklin, more than a little peeved at this outsider's inability to see the order of things in Banfield. "This is *our* school. You serve at our pleasure. You seem to misunder—"

"This is the community's school, Franklin. I apologize for interrupting you, but this is not your school. It is not Mary George Taskill's school. This isn't the senator's school. I work as the board's one employee, and for no board member individually. Everyone else here works for me. All teachers and all staff work for me. All students work for their teachers and for their parents, as they gather the growth and wisdom that comes with becoming a quality human being. This issue of these boys behaving cruelly and crassly from computer terminals or smartphones instead of the lunch line threatens to diminish their development as quality human beings, if we fail to educate them at this teachable moment, and if their parents fail to do the same in *partnership* with the school. Frankly, Franklin, this is why trustees go through orientation prior to becoming trustees. I need and expect your support."

The headmaster crossed his legs so comfortably that Franklin felt his blood boil. What an impudent god-damned Atlanta jackass. This was the problem with Banfield these days. All these know-it-alls moving to town telling you what to do and how to raise your children. This son of a bitch needed a major attitude adjustment, something these Atlanta jackasses probably called a "comeuppance" or some such.

"So you're not going to apologize?" Franklin asked in a tone which he hoped conveyed trouble for Paul Garrett.

"Not for doing my job."

Franklin leaned forward. "You're deliberately disobeying a board directive, Paul."

The headmaster uncrossed his legs and leaned forward. Franklin could have punched him in the face.

"There is no board directive, Franklin. You would have to call a board meeting, establish a quorum, introduce a motion, and cite policy in discussion prior to a vote to change the board by-laws to state that the board runs day-to-day operations of the school, including the character education of the students. Is that what you want to do? Or do you want to support my authority and judgment in teaching children that kindness and respect are expected at all times, even when sitting in their bedrooms writing to and about each other on such a public platform as

Facebook. Go ahead. In the meantime," said the headmaster as he rose to his feet and extended his hand, "I have much to do before the end of the school day."

Furious, Franklin Redstone stood, hating the fact that he was a few inches shorter than this Atlanta know-it-all. He shook the headmaster's hand with every bit of strength he could muster.

"I expect you to follow the directive I gave you in the email this morning, Paul."

The board chairman exited swiftly, commenting to the receptionist that he hoped she would have a good afternoon. He was out the door before he could hear her response, his cell phone receiving a flurry of punches en route to his cream-colored Escalade.

***

An hour after his chat with Franklin Redstone, Paul Garrett sat on an old metal folding chair at the north end of the soccer field. It was an Indian summer October afternoon in the Lowcountry, and already he was wiping perspiration from his brow and chin. He loosened his striped tie slightly to let his neck breathe, keeping the tie in rough position for the two committee meetings which would follow this collaboration with the four eighth-grade boys.

The boys were already making excellent progress. The first of two red wheelbarrows was already a quarter full, the short but stubborn weeds accumulating with every careful drop made by each of the four students.

The headmaster pointed to his left. "Billy, grab that candy wrapper over there, will you?"

Billy Painter, kneeling over a troublesome patch of weed moss, looked in the direction indicated by the headmaster's forefinger.

"What candy wrapper, Mr. G?" he asked earnestly.

"Well, Billy, if you get up and investigate, I promise you'll find something."

Billy, a rangy, athletic boy with close-cropped brown hair, clambered to his feet and began walking in small ovals until he found something. He bent over and picked up a small triangular piece of flimsy plastic, about an inch in length, and held it up for the headmaster to see.

"Is this what you mean, Mr. G?"

"Sure is, Bill. Well done! Back to it now."

Billy placed the piece of torn-off candy-bar wrapper into the wheelbarrow and resumed his position picking at the weed moss.

"Mr. Garrett?"

Paul looked to his right to find that Charles Taskill had risen to his knees with a handful of weeds.

"Yes, Charles?"

"That wasn't a candy wrapper, Mr. Garrett. It was just the little piece you tear off to be able to eat the candy bar. You said we were pulling weeds, and then could go home, but now you say Billy has to pick up trash, and that's not even trash. Whoever ate that candy bar threw the big part of the wrapper away like they're supposed to. And even if it *is* trash, why should *we* have to pick it up? Whoever left it gets away with it, but we have to pick it up? That's not fair! None of this is fair!"

"Why isn't it fair, Charles?" the headmaster asked.

Charles threw the weeds onto the ground but remained on his knees.

"Because none of us did anything wrong here at school. Right, guys?"

The other three boys kept at the weeds, glancing furtively at the headmaster. Billy answered the question quietly. "Right."

Charles, emboldened by Billy's confirmation, said "*See,* Mr.

Garrett? This isn't fair! We didn't do anything wrong at school. We all did it at home. My mom says that isn't your, your... your jooris... dexshun..."

Paul decided to help the boy out. "Do you mean 'jurisdiction,' Charles?"

"Yeah! That's it! My mom says we can sue you for making me come to your office, and for making us do hard labor when we didn't do anything wrong."

"Well, Charles, your mom is a smart lady, so I'm not going to talk about what she says, okay?"

Charles looked surprised, and looked around at his schoolmates. "Um. Okay."

"So I want to talk about what *you* have said. How's that sound?"

"Okay." Charles went back to work on the weeds, picking up the small pile in front of him, rising to deposit it into the wheelbarrow, and returning to his spot.

"Charles, I don't want to be unfair. Do all you guys understand that?"

There was a full round of affirmative responses, with a couple of 'sirs' thrown in.

"Okay. Thanks, guys. So Charles, when you said you're doing hard labor for not doing anything wrong, do you mean that?"

"About the hard labor?"

"Charles."

"Okay, sir. Sorry. Um. Yes."

"You think you didn't do anything wrong."

"No, sir. I mean, yes, I did something wrong, but I didn't do it *here*."

"Okay, Charles, so you did do something wrong. Was it mean?"

"Yes, sir."

"Was it ugly?"

"Um. Yes, sir."

"Was it meant to hurt somebody else?"

"Well, not on purpose."

"Charles."

"Yes, sir."

"*Was* it on purpose?"

"Um. Yes, sir."

"But you did it at home, in your bedroom, at your computer."

"Yes, sir! I did it *there*."

"So I should say it's okay for you to be a student here even if you want to be mean, ugly and deliberately hurtful to other people in the community, as long as you do it at home or in restaurants or other places like that."

Charles looked around at the others. Their heads were down, intent upon the work at hand.

"Mr. Garrett, I didn't say I want to be all those things," Charles said quietly.

"Charles, if you don't want to be all those things, then don't do them at home on your computer. You sent messages to the whole world, Charles, through cyberspace, that you want to be all those things. And you, Eric. And you, Carter. And you, Billy. You called other people names that I don't think you'd use in front of me or in front of your parents. You used language that is disgusting, offensive and ignorant in every way. If you called me those names right now, what do you think would happen?"

In unison the boys replied "We'd be expelled."

"Yes, I'm afraid so, boys. I would have no choice, because you know better than that. But let me ask you this. If you had written those messages on the campus computers instead of at home, what do you think I would have done?"

Charles offered an answer. "Expelled us?"

"No, Charles. I don't think you'd learn anything from that. No, I wouldn't have expelled you boys. But if you want, I'll tell you what I would have done."

Billy raised his hand as if in class. "What, Mr. G?" he asked eagerly.

Ah, thought Paul to himself. These really are great kids.

Paul leaned forward as if sharing a deep secret. The boys, all four of them, did likewise, as if surrounding a campfire.

Paul looked around to make sure nobody else was eavesdropping on the conversation.

"First, I would have made you come to my office, all four of you. And then…"

"Yeah?" came the excited response from all four boys, but not in unison. Charles Taskill's fervent 'yeah?' came first.

"Then I would have had a good conversation with you about what was wrong with doing what you did. And *then*…"

Silence was interrupted only by the soft whisk of the afternoon breeze and the cars passing by on the street about a hundred yards away.

"… I would have made you pull weeds with me on the soccer field."

The boys kept staring intently, waiting for something more.

Billy Painter broke the silence. "But, but that's what we're doing now. That whole thing's what happened already!"

The other boys started laughing. So did the headmaster.

"Now why would it be the same, boys? Seriously, think about it. Why would it be the same?"

Charles raised his hand.

"Yes, Charles?"

"Because what we did wrong would've been the same?"

"Outstanding, young man!" The headmaster rose to his feet and invited the boys to do the same, staying in the tight campfire-style circle. The boys beamed, grinning at each other as the headmaster shook their hands.

"But wait a second, guys. If what you did wrong was the same, and if the consequences would have been the same, does it matter *where* you did something wrong, or *whether* you did something wrong?"

In unison again, the boys said "Whether!"

"Excellent. Now keep something in mind about who you are, and what and who you want to become. 'Character is what you do and who you are when *nobody* is looking.'"

"Even in our rooms," said Eric Horton.

"Especially in your rooms," said Paul Garrett.

The boys went back to their work without being asked. Paul Garrett hunched up his khaki slacks and joined them on his knees, holding up a large chunk of ugly weed moss and proclaiming himself the weed-pulling champion of Saxby Academy. A round cry of enthusiastic dissent arose from the four busy young men around him, prompting the headmaster to withdraw an Eisenhower silver dollar from his right front pants pocket. Displaying it in his open palm, he dared three young men to outweed the 'old champion.'

As he sank back down to increase his lead in the competition, his cell phone pinged. He pulled it from his left pocket. The screen revealed a text from Franklin Redstone. The board was calling a special session tonight at six. Could Paul arrive ten minutes early?

The headmaster smiled, shook his head, and sent a quick text to his wife that he would be unavoidably late for dinner.

ANNIVERSARY

✳ ✳ ✳

I stared at him. He averted his eyes, of course. Locked his eyes on his penny loafers, the old black ones with the worn-out heels. That's what cowards and lousy dads and unfaithful husbands do. They hide their eyes in their shoes. When they lie.

The thing about saying he had sent me flowers "lots of times, baby," when I can count to two perfectly well and I know how to stop if something never gets to three, is that he had the chance to say he never bought HER flowers. "Not once," he could have said. "Because she isn't you, baby," he could have said. "She could never be you. Because there's only one you, baby, and there ain't a candle in the world she could hold next to you..."

But he didn't say that. He said, "But Emma, I've sent you flowers too, like, lots of times, and I love you. It was just an accident. A one-time thing. Please. You shouldn't feel bad. It wasn't your fault." And then he averted those eyes and looked at those shitty old shoes and I knew it wasn't an accident.

So I decided to go see this girl, this new 'baby' whose address was put on the sender lines by the florist instead of on the recipient ones. Lonnie. Some kind of redneck name. Probably short for Lonette or some such. Bless her heart. She didn't know about me, I'm sure. Sort of like that Amber Frey woman that was so enamored with that lizard named Scott Peterson. Anyways, so I get to 249 Travers Lane and take the deepest breath of my life. I push the doorbell and it ding-dongs inside and I think about running away like a kid on a prank. But I stand there, all resolute, and wait, surprised by my courage, or maybe disgusted that I even care about a woman who jumps right in the sack just because an uninspired man like my husband sends her flowers.

So the door opens and there's this man, this poor sap who clearly doesn't know about the fling his wife is having with my husband. Or maybe he did. He had a sad look on his face. His mustache looked wet, sort of like he'd been crying. Still, I said I wanted to talk to Lonnie right freaking now. A dark expression entered his eyes. "I'm Lonnie," he said.

I stared at him. "What did you say?"

"I'm Lonnie," he said. "And you're Emma."

Well, I tell you honestly, I was speechless. I gathered my strength and took an even deeper breath than the one thirty seconds ago. When I spoke, I knew my life was going to change forever.

"Lonnie. Are you... in love with my husband?"

Lonnie stood there. He looked in my eyes, like he was searching for something. I don't know whether he found it, but then he spoke, almost in a whisper.

"Emma, I know who you are."

I took a step back. "No," I said. "You don't."

"Emma, we miss Janie. Today's the anniversary. You know that."

The poor man was crazy. Don't you see he was crazy? I decided to leave. I almost made it down the steps.

"Emma, it wasn't your fault."

I stopped and turned around on the bottom porch step.

"We believe that, Emma. We know that. We really do. You know, Barb and I always take pictures of the flowers from you and Bob. Every year we take pictures. We pretend the flowers live forever with us. It means a lot. We forgave you a long time ago, Emma. It happens every day in America. Janie ran out for the ball, and you—"

"Tell your wife to leave my husband alone!" I said. He was a clueless sack, changing the subject like that.

"Emma, please. You've got to see someone."

"Tell your wife to stay away from my husband or I will KILL her. What kind of name is Lonnie for a woman anyway?"

I got him good on that one. He was married to a floozy who couldn't leave the neighborhood men alone. He looked down at his shoes, just like my husband. He was a defeated man. I could go now.

As I stepped over the curb to cross the street and walk the four blocks back to our corner of Spruce and Travers, I felt sorry for the poor man. He just didn't know about his wife. I've heard it said if she'd been a better mother their daughter would still be alive. Sure, they can sit there and eat their Cheerios together every morning, but they're over. Bob and I, though? We'll recover, because that's what full-on love does. It comes back. It remembers the good things. It forgets Lonnie, just like it forgets bad mothers who don't keep their Janies in the yard. Love roars back, sending bunches and bunches of flowers.

And it will not be interrupted by memories of bad things.

THE MURDER OF
EFREM LAFFITTE

✻ ✻ ✻

opper Smalls awoke to the screams of his wife. Terrified that Master Efrem was taking a liking to Hannah like the one he had that afternoon two years ago, Copper heaved himself up from the sweat-soiled bed and rushed to the front porch of the tiny cabin. The agony in Hannah's wailing, coming from somewhere outside near the barn, brought back the searing lashes of pain which would forever criss-cross Copper's back.

His bare feet carrying him down the three decrepit steps to the dusty compound, Copper saw Hannah on her knees, sobbing into the apron of Jazie the cook. Copper thanked God as he hurried toward his wife. Thank God she wasn't in the barn. Thank God she wasn't screaming at Master Efrem to get off of her. Thank God that Copper wasn't running up from the field to put a stop to it and buy another thirty lashes. Something was wrong, but Thank God, he thought. Thank *God*.

Reaching his wife, Copper looked at Jazie as he laid a gentle right hand on Hannah's quivering shoulder.

"Whuz happened?"

Jazie, who had the red eyes of one who had been crying herself, looked with resigned surprise at Copper. "You mean, you don't know neithah? Oh mah Lawd. Mah Lawd, mah Lawd, mah Lawd."

Copper opened his mouth and stared at Jazie, who was shaking her head almost to the rhythm of Hannah's bobbing sobs.

"Jazie, don't keep nothin' from me now," said Copper in his deep cracked voice. "Whuz got my wife so shot up with emotion?"

Before Jazie could speak, Hannah looked up and screamed again. Then she stood and placed her shaky palms on Copper's stubbled cheeks.

"Coppuh, it's Fathuh Abraham. He's—he's…"

"Dead." The voice came from behind Copper. "Guess there *is* a God after all, jes' like Reverend James's been tellin' all you niggers."

Copper turned slowly, taking his wife's wrists to remove her palms from his cheeks. He faced the red-headed white man, whose long wild beard featured a dozen or so breadcrumbs.

"Fathuh Abraham ain't dead, Massuh Efrem. Doan you speak dat way. Please doan you speak dat way."

Efrem Laffitte, thirty-one years old and the eldest son of the plantation owners, George and Frances Laffitte, was not about to take instruction from an old field slave like Copper Smalls.

"I'll speak to you that way, Copper, you goddamned nigger, any time I right-wise feel like it." Efrem took a step toward Copper. Hannah sniffled and tried to pull her husband back.

Efrem pointed at Copper. "I'll speak that way 'cause I'm damn glad that nigger-lovin' president a yours got his. Sure, you gonna be free, Copper Smalls, but you ain't gonna be safe and you ain't gonna eat. Nigger-lovin' president ain't gonna be around no more to take care uh you and your stinkin' kind."

Master Efrem took another step, within a yard of Copper and his wife. Copper heard Jazie shuffle backward, but held his gaze on Master Efrem.

"Efrem Laffitte, you a mean man," growled Copper. "If Fathuh Abraham is gone, you shouldn' go an' wet on him. No suh."

Copper's gut churned, his throat swelling with grief. He turned toward Jazie.

"Whuz happened? How'd he—"

"He got his head shot off by a *patriot*. That's what happened, son!" Efrem poked Copper on his left shoulder and grinned. "Patriot which goes by the name uh Booth."

Copper jerked his arm away from Master Efrem. "I *ain't* yo *son*."

Efrem lost his grin. "Oh, you're my son all right. You're my *boy*, son. Jes' like yer wife's still my *whore*. Jes' like—"

The next word never left Master Efrem's mouth. Copper released Hannah and thrust both hands viselike over Efrem Laffitte's bearded throat. Driving his legs forward, Copper rode Master Efrem to the ground, squeezing with all his might, ignoring the white man's panicked gurgling. Copper stared sightlessly into Master Efrem's bulging eyes, oblivious to the clawing of two women trying to save Copper's life by saving their master's. He'd been emancipated, they'd said. A pretty long time ago, they'd said. Only thing was, Master Efrem and his mommy and daddy had never told them. Never told them they could go. Never told them they were free. And now this bastard blasphemes Father Abraham. Speaks of raping Hannah and...

Copper heard something that sounded like Hannah, the begging, sobbing sound of her voice from a distance, getting closer and closer until Copper found himself gazing at the cold, surprised, fixed still eyes of Master Efrem Laffitte.

***

Night fell upon Copper Smalls like a heavy black cloak. He was tempted to rest, as he no longer heard the baying hounds and the shouts of their masters. His masters.

His exhaustion frightened him. His forties had dawned three years ago, and he had fallen unconscious from the heat in the cotton field three times last summer. But autumn brought relief, and on many days in October his energy had allowed him to meet the masters' minimum harvests without a whipping. Unfortunately the heat was early this spring. It arrived in March. March in Georgia normally energized him for the backbreaking work in the field, but this March had brought a hot sun and a humid air. Now, with April providing no relief and the awful news of the murder of Father Abraham, with all his remaining days condemned to the hunt, he was the most unfortunate of black men: sixty in his forties, the killer of a white man of landed gentry, the widower or fugitive husband of a tortured woman, all ironically on the heels of the news of his freedom and the end of the war.

His temper had gotten the best of him before; he had the ravaged map of scars on his back to prove it. And now his days were few, or one, or less than one. He *must* have at least one. And then at least another. And another…until he found either his wife or Jesus.

He emerged from the forest, searching for signs of life, a campfire, a light in a window, the shadowy movement of livestock, any sign that might either threaten his life or provide sanctuary, or perhaps leave him in the middle fields of indifference. Legs wobbly from dehydrated fatigue, Copper scaled a small weedy hill, tripping in the dark over exposed old roots and snake holes in the dry dirt. He kept tripping, getting up, tripping, getting up, until he reached the top of the hill. He stopped and gazed at the cloud-obscured glow of the moon. Where should he go? Did he have time to rest?

As if in answer, the return of the faint baying of hounds penetrated his drained awareness, jerking him back to the alertness which would have to be his closest friend for the rest of his life.

He must keep going. God would see to his survival. But he

must *deserve* God's help. He would not stay alive if he rested. God did not want him to sleep.

God had never wanted Copper to be free, Copper remembered as he strode carefully across the uneven terrain of unclaimed acreage which did not appear to end in the dark horizon ahead of him. He must especially remember that now. God had always wanted him to survive. After all, he was forty-three. At twenty-three Copper never spent a minute considering the possibility of forty-three, nor had he wanted to. God had wanted him to survive. God had *made* him survive. In Copper there had been no choice. God had made him live. Had made him work. Had made him know of the rape of his wife by Efrem Laffitte. Oh Lord, why did he have to *KNOW?*

And now God made him know even more. That he had been free already, pulling his burdens in the fields of masters who knew the truth and hid it. The truth that Father Abraham was dead. Why did Copper have to know *this?* Father Abraham was *dead?* Copper could have lived the rest of his days without knowing that Father Abraham was dead. That would have suited him fine, because the Hope was what sustained him, sustained all of them, this love from a man they had never met. It was the love of Jesus. Copper was sure of it. He was not a church man, in spite of the Laffittes requiring all slaves to attend services on the plantation every Wednesday night and Sunday morning. But he *was* a Jesus man. Yes, sir. And so was Father Abraham. Yes, sir. If Father Abraham was dead, then so was Jesus, and so was God. After making Copper survive, that was. God would finish making Copper survive, and then God would finish dying too.

He had to stop thinking about God. Jazie the cook said that just last week, while ladling boiled potatoes onto Copper's tin plate. "Lawd, Coppuh, you got ta stop thinkin' bout God. God ain't thinkin' bout you." Copper had looked at Jazie, stern as he could muster, and said, "I think about Father Abraham. I forgot God a long time ago."

"I knows you did, Coppuh. Now if Fathuh Abraham thinks about you, you got sumphun dere. Mebbe Fathuh Abraham is God. Then we could all hope."

Copper had laughed. And then he had stopped.

Up ahead he saw a light glow in the darkness, faint in the distance, like a lit firefly resting on a post. It didn't move, so it wasn't a campfire. Was it a house? A hanging lantern? He had to know. If it housed indifference or sanctuary, it was a light to move toward. If it was a threat, it couldn't be a greater one than the growing sound of hounds back on his scent. He tried to run. He could not. He would count his steps. He could make it there, one step at a time. He guessed it would take five hundred.

It took four hundred and seventy six to reach the point where he could see that the light was on the second floor of a house. He could make out a chimney against the cover of clouds in the night sky. No smoke billowed or wisped. They weren't cooking inside. Nor of course were they cold. They might be indifferent, but they were not cold. Not this April. Not this year.

When he had moved close enough to see that the house was sided in wide wood planks, unpainted, he was relieved. He had never seen an unpainted house inhabited by slave-owners. This was not a plantation house. There were no outbuildings. No barn. Only the outhouse off to the right. There were no other houses nearby. No evidence of crops or furrowed fields. Someone was home, but there were no horses. This home belonged to someone who worked for someone else.

A chance for sanctuary? Or at the least, indifference? He decided to find out.

There was no light downstairs. Upstairs the light flickered, imperceptible from five hundred strides, but now it was clear that candlelight interrupted the darkness in a room on the second floor. Someone was home.

Again he heard the baying of hounds, maybe a thousand strides away. His legs were cramping, his head was heavy, and his clothes weighed three times as much wet from sweat as they did dry. If he kept going, unable to run, judgment and focus clouded by fatigue and hunger and parched throat, in an hour the thousand strides would be ten. In two he would be dead, hanging from the limb of a tree, beaten and mocked before wetting himself struggling at the end of a rope that was too short to mercifully break his neck. He would knock on this door. God would help him survive. And then God would die too.

He stepped gingerly onto the first wooden step of the uncovered front porch. It did not creak. Neither did the second. Maybe the resident was a carpenter. The steps were solid. Copper tested the third riser, the fourth, the fifth. He inhaled and held his breath, ascending onto the porch. He could make out the front door, several feet ahead. It had a large knocker. He reached for it, then hesitated. What if this was a slave owner? A friend of the Laffittes? He turned and looked out over the open portions of the property. Still seeing no shapes resembling outbuildings that might be slave quarters, he exhaled slowly, as if the residents of the house could hear him breathe. He was convinced that they could. Surely the approaching hounds could, and would adjust their course with even greater accuracy.

Copper made his decision for the second time, this time with the resolve born of necessity and its erratic cousin, panic. He banged the knocker twice against the thick oak door, eased it quietly back against the wood, and stepped back a pace, heart pounding in his chest and temples.

He heard the release of a latch. The door creaked open to reveal first a candle, then its holder. It was a boy, not older than seven or eight, in a long nightshirt and bare feet. His hair appeared to be black in the dim candlelight.

"Who are you?" the boy said.

"My name, sir, is Copper Smalls. I'm lookin' for a place to stay for a few hours. Is your father home?"

The boy regarded Copper, his face aglow from the candle, the flickering shadows making his eyes look expressionlessly mysterious.

"I don't have a father. He was shot."

"Oh. I'm sorry." Copper turned toward the darkness behind him. The dogs' baying was getting closer. "May I speak to your mother?"

"Papa was shot at Antietam."

"I'm very sorry. Your mother may be able to—"

"But the gangrene killed him. You're a nigger, aren't you?"

"Well, I'm… yes. From the Laffitte plantation. Do you know the Laffittes?"

"My papa had to fight instead of the Laffittes. They paid the special tax. Papa went in their place."

Copper knew he had only minutes to be inside and persuade the boy's mother to hide him. If this family resented the Laffittes, the mother might cooperate if she knew Copper was on the run.

"May I come in and speak to your mother?"

"I ain't got no mother. Mama died when I was born. But you can come in and talk to Darla." The boy took a step back.

"Thank you, sir. Who is Darla?"

"My sister. She takes care of me and Rupert."

Copper entered and closed the front door.

"Darla must be wonderful. Where might we find her? I'm in a terrible hurry, sir."

"Why do you call me that?"

"Why? Well. I'm a slave. And you're not."

"I ain't no nigger either, boy." The child said the words without contempt, as if he had only heard them without practicing them.

"Robert!" a voice hissed from the top of the stairs. It was a female voice. She carried no candle, but Copper could make her out, standing on the landing in what appeared to be a wide nightgown.

"Sister, this nigger wants to hide here," called the boy. "He's runnin' from the Laffittes."

The girl took two steps downward and stopped.

"I apologize for my little brother. He's never met a black man before. Just knows what you get called is all."

She took another descending step and halted once again.

"Are you one of the Laffittes' slaves?"

"Yes, ma'am. My name's Copper. Copper Smalls. The men with the dogs is after me. I did somethin' bad. May I hide here?"

"They will come to our door, Mister Smalls."

Nobody in Copper's forty-three years had ever addressed him as Mister Smalls. He wasn't sure what to say. And then he heard the dogs again. They were no more than a hundred yards away, heading straight for the house.

"I know they'll come to your door, ma'am. May I hide upstairs? Or wherever you say?"

Suddenly she descended the stairs as quickly as she could, breathing audibly, nervously.

"Give me your shirt, Mister Smalls. I'll throw it out back for the dogs to discover. They might think you removed it and kept runnin'. Jacob, take Mister Smalls to the fruit cellar. Go down and hide with him. Hurry!" She stood before Copper, and took the candle from the boy.

"My name is Darla, Mister Smalls. I'm fifteen. This is my house. I won't let them in. I promise. My papa is dead because of them."

Copper stared into the glow that danced on her face. Her hair was down, shoulder length, dark like her brother's. The light revealed a kindness in her eyes, something he'd never seen in the eyes of a white person looking at him.

"Thank—"

"Go!" she hissed.

The boy grabbed Copper by the hand and led him into the darkness of a hallway. At the end of the hall the boy opened a creaky door and led Copper down onto the first wooden step. Copper reached back and pulled the door shut behind them. The blackness was total. The boy pulled him down, step by step, Copper counting ten before they set foot on what felt like clay on his bare feet.

"Let's sit," whispered the boy. "If they come in we can hide behind my papa's old table. Back in the corner."

Copper allowed the boy to pull him down into a sitting position. They were both still. The silence rang loud in his ears. He did not want to hang. Not without seeing his wife again.

As if his thoughts had been shouted aloud, the heavy knocker upstairs was employed, with great aggression, at least ten times. Copper heard Darla yell, "Coming!" There was a disdain in her tone, which Copper, and perhaps the girl, hoped would send the men along on account of their rudeness, or perhaps the lateness of the hour.

But these hunters were slave-owners, or drew their livings in slave-owners' employ. There were five rungs in Southern society, Copper knew. At the top were the planters, like the Laffittes. All laws and representation were for their service and benefit. At the second level were the men who worked for, or provided goods and services to, the planters. Sometimes these were men who owned slaves if they could afford them. Then there were men who performed labor for the aristocracy for a wage, and men who owned and worked small farms but couldn't afford anything more than livestock, falling short of slave-ownership and the minimal housing and feeding requirements of owning human livestock. The rung below this one consisted of white women who weren't married to, or the offspring of, the planters. This societal level was inhabited by Darla, and before that by Darla's mother.

These men were not going to be concerned about waking this household, especially if they already knew that this girl-woman of fifteen was the head of it. The pounding resumed. The door opened. Copper could hear the panting of dogs. And then came the voices.

"Sorry to bother you, Darla. We're looking for one of our niggers." The voice was familiar. It was Efrem Laffitte's younger brother, Arthur. Arthur was the father of Jazie the cook's little girl. Copper remembered that Jazie's husband, Copper's close friend Octavius, got thirty lashes for challenging Arthur to a fair honor fight. This was before Copper's own wife was violated by Efrem.

"Mister Arthur, there ain't been no niggers this way, far as I know."

Copper squeezed his eyes shut in the pitch black. *Please, God. Reward this child's courage.*

"Far as you know, Darla? Far as you know? Far as I know, you'd lie to me for a slice of apple. Where's that little brother of yours?"

"He's sleeping, Mister Arthur. If you and your dogs haven't woken him."

"The hounds say the nigger's here, Darla. Look at 'em. They want to go down that there hallway. How about we just—"

"I will give you permission, Mister Arthur, to look out back first. I know I heard somethin' about five minutes ago, up in the tree by my window."

"Listen to you, now." Arthur laughed. "So now you think you heard a nigger?"

"No. I thought I heard a cat."

Silence ensued. Copper counted to eight Mississippi before he heard Arthur reply.

"Okay. We'll take the dogs out back. But I'm leavin' Jarrod here. In case you got the nigger ready to run back out the door. You clever bitch."

"Whatever you say, Mister Arthur. I ain't interested in no runaway slaves no how. Go check and come back. Search the house. I don't care. I just want to go back to bed."

Copper heard the door shut as the sound of panting dogs stopped. Again the silence rang loud in his ears. He took the hand of the boy. He felt the tremble there. The boy whispered: "I know where my papa kept his shotgun, the one he used for venison."

Copper's heart leapt. "Shhh. Quiet now. We might not need it." He paused, then risked one more whisper, hopefully inaudible to Jarrod Laffitte, the youngest of Efrem's siblings. "Is it far?"

"No," came the whispered reply. "It's under these stairs. It's loaded."

"How, how do you know that?"

"Cuz that's how Papa kept it. He left it here cuz the army gave him a rifle that shoots mini balls."

"Jacob. Do you know exactly where it is under the stairs?"

"Yes."

"Can you get it without knocking anything over?"

"I think so."

"Okay. Get it."

The boy let go of Copper's hand and shuffled around the left side of the stairs. Silence.

"Do you have it?" Copper whispered.

"Yes."

"Good. Bring it here."

Silence.

"Jacob?"

Silence.

"Jacob, bring it here."

"Mister Smalls?"

"Yes, Jacob. Whisper, now. Bring me the gun."

"Mister Smalls, do you think there's a reward for your capture?"

Ice shot through Copper's veins. He had to be careful with his words. This boy was being taken care of by a fifteen-year-old girl pretending in the world to be twenty. Money was surely lacking in this household.

"Oh, I doubt it, Jacob. But we have to stop talkin'. They might hear us. Just bring me the gun, Jacob." It was a challenge not to use his voice, but the boy's shift of perspective was alarming.

"The Merrifields got two hundred dollars for turning in Averil, that runaway from the Carraway plantation. You think Darla and I could get two hundred for you?"

"Jacob, are you pointing that gun at me? Don't cock it. They'd hear it upstairs for sure."

"Just speculatin', sir." The boy's whisper hung in the air like a dissipating mist.

Silence continued from upstairs, and then Copper heard the door burst open followed by Arthur Laffitte bellowing, "Copper took off his shirt! Behind the house! Must've taken off up in them woods back there. Sorry, Darla. We's goin' now."

Copper suppressed a giddy urge to snicker; Darla was brilliant.

"Sorry for wakin' you, Darla. Glad you wasn't lyin'. You'd a been in a heap a trouble."

"I'm glad too," Darla said, her voice sounding far more compliant as the men exited and the door creaked shut.

Copper heaved a sigh of relief, but it was interrupted by the sound of the front door creaking back open upstairs.

"Arthur!" called Darla.

"Yes, Darla!" came the distant reply.

"Is there going to be a reward for the nigger if we see him?"

"Yes! A hunnerd dollars!"

"Okay, Arthur! We'll keep an eye out! Sure could use a hundred dollars!"

Again the door creaked shut.

"Jacob," Copper said, using his full voice. "Give me the shotgun. Let me buy it."

"With what? Niggers don't have no money."

"I promise to—"

The door swung open at the top of the stairs.

"They've gone!" Darla called down.

"Jacob's got the shotgun on me, Darla," Copper said as he advanced to the steps. "Please. They'd hang me as an example to the rest. Is that worth a hundred dollars?"

Darla laughed. "Please. I was just funnin' that awful man so's he would think I'm on his side or just want money like any normal human bein'. Jacob, give our new friend the gun."

Copper accepted the shotgun from the boy, who clambered up the stairs ahead of the black man.

"I was just funnin' the nigger, Darla!" Jacob exclaimed, giggling. "Fooled him too!"

Copper reached the top of the steps and laughed. "You surely did, Jacob. You surely did."

"You'd best keep movin', Mister Smalls," Darla said, gesturing toward the door. "But first let me get you a jug a water and some bread. You can take it with you."

Darla hurried down the narrow dark hall to what Copper presumed must be a small kitchen. He looked down at the boy.

"You and your sister are angels, Jacob."

"Don't know if I'm an angel, mister nigger. But my sister is. We's goin' to pray for you."

"Is this shotgun really loaded, Jacob?"

Jacob smiled. "No, sir. We needed some venison last month. I used Papa's gun. It weren't shot after he died and didn't never come home. Till last month that is. I got lucky. We been eatin' good."

Darla reappeared with half a loaf of baked bread and an earthen jug with a small handle and round top.

"Here you go, Mister Smalls. Safe travels. We'll be prayin' for you."

"I was just tellin' your brother that you're angels. Thank you, ma'am."

Copper set down the unloaded shotgun. It was of no use to him. Carrying the bread in his left hand and the jug hanging from his right forefinger, Copper moved to the door, which the boy opened for him.

"Wait!" Darla said. "You need a shirt. One of my father's. Papa was your size, and his shirt don't smell like what those hounds are lookin' for." Darla ran back down the hall and around the corner. She returned in a few seconds with a white long-sleeved button-up shirt. Copper handed the bread and water jug to Darla while he donned and buttoned up the shirt. He rolled the sleeves up to his elbows and reached for the bread and jug, when Darla again said "Wait!" and ran around the corner again.

She returned with a pair of laced brown shoes. Copper tried on the left one. It fit, as did the right.

"Angels," he said, accepting the bread and jug again. "There are white angels," he whispered. "White angels." Darla stepped forward and kissed Copper on the right cheek. Jacob stood resolutely at the open door. As Copper stepped out into the night, he looked down at the boy and smiled.

"Son," he said. "Be like Father Abraham when you grow up. Your sister already is."

Copper descended the front steps, looked over his shoulder at the two white angels, and took his own advice. He started walking back in the direction from which he had come. His freedom, after all, would become his prison if his wife remained in Hell.

CRAWDAD CREEK

* * *

"So if Mr. Morgan leaves Elkton at two o'clock, and Mr. Allen leaves Littlefield at two-twenty, what time will each of them…"

Mrs. Dixon droned on, providing speeds, distances, et cetera for the math problem as Cole Reed reached across the aisle to his left and flipped a folded piece of paper onto Bobby Shuster's desk. Bobby looked cautiously toward the blackboard, then opened the note.

Who gives a crap? the note read in Cole's loopy scrawl.

Bobby smiled, glanced furtively at the teacher's back, and jotted a response on the same sheet of paper. Cole opened and read Bobby's message:

Mrs. Dixon's mama.

Cole let out an involuntary snort as he choked back a laugh. Mrs. Dixon spun from the board to face the class, just as every student, nearly twenty of them, straightened attentively in an act of solidarity to conceal the laugher's identity.

"Would someone like to share with all of us what he or she finds so amusing about the journeys of Mr. Morgan and Mr. Allen?"

Mrs. Dixon swept her stare across the classroom for a few seconds, then turned back to the blackboard.

"So if Mr. Morgan's average rate of speed for the first leg of the trip…"

Cole immediately wrote and delivered his reply to Bobby:

Bet you'd like to share something amusing with Mrs. Dixon.

Bobby smiled, whipped out a response, and deposited it on Cole's desk:

Like your willie. If she can find it.

"…and so turn to page 266 for an explanation of how we find the answer."

All of the students except Cole and Bobby turned dutifully to page 266 as Cole wrote furiously, Bobby craning his neck for an advance view of Cole's comeback. Cole covered the words with his forearm like protecting a test from the wandering eyes of a cheater, and then passed the note back to Bobby.

To find it she'd have to go to your mama's house.

Bobby leaned over to glare at Cole, who let out another snort a half-second before he could clap both hands over his mouth. Mrs. Dixon turned in time to see Bobby struggle to resume his upright position.

"Mr. Shuster." All eyes focused on Bobby, his face rapidly flushing red. "Mr. Shuster, since you obviously find this problem amusing in its simplicity, perhaps you'd like to come to the board and explain the solution we just found."

Bobby stared first at Mrs. Dixon, and then at Cole, who was bent studiously over his now-open textbook.

"Today, Mr. Shuster."

Bobby stood and advanced to the board with his book, looking back twice at Cole, who was reviewing the material with utmost seriousness.

"Students who find math funny must also find it easy, Mr. Shuster. Beginning with Mr. Morgan in Elkton and Mr. Allen in Littlefield, please solve the problem of arrival times, and show all your steps please."

Bobby was incredulous. He glared back at Cole again, but without the satisfaction, meager though it would have been, of eye contact with the instigator of the trouble he now inhabited.

"All my steps?"

"All of them, Mr. Shuster. Perhaps you'll even have time to tell us which step you found so hilarious."

Bobby stared futilely at his open book.

"What *page* are we on, Mr. Shuster?"

It was a rhetorical question. Mrs. Dixon turned to face the class. "Would anyone like to show Mr. Shuster the solution to this problem? Someone who has been paying attention?"

Several students raised their hands, but Cole Reed's stood out as most confident.

"Mr. Reed. Thank you."

Cole carried his book to the board, careful to avoid eye contact with Bobby.

"Before Mr. Reed begins, Mr. Shuster, please return to your seat. I suggest that you think about what kind of student you want to be."

Bobby completed the interminable walk of shame back to his desk. He picked up his pen and scribbled on the note which had been originated by his best friend, who was now reaping Mrs. Dixon's praise in the background of Bobby's consciousness.

***

The final bell rang, its shrillness lasting until the front doors of the school opened and kids streamed out and down the brick steps to the front campus lawn. Among them were Bobby and Cole. They reached the sidewalk bordering Academy Avenue and turned right, kicking stones as they went.

"So how much?" Bobby said.

"Five bucks," Cole replied.

"Five *bucks?* You got five bucks? I bet you don't have five bucks."

"I got five bucks. Least, I can get it if Foreman wins."

"If Foreman wins, don't go stiffin' me like you did in Dixon's class today. Asswipe."

Cole laughed. "You shoulda seen your face! That was hilarious. But don't worry, I can get five bucks from my mom if I have to. Which I won't 'cause Ali's gonna kick that black guy's ass."

"Black guy? What in the world do you think Ali is?"

"Ali ain't black. He's Muslim. He used to be black."

Bobby stopped. "What? Do you know how stupid that is?"

"Who was stupid when I nailed that problem in Dixon's class? *Mister* Shuster."

"That's bullshit," Bobby said as they resumed walking. "You wouldn't be anywhere in that class if it wasn't for me. Dumbass," he added, delivering a playful punch to Cole's right shoulder.

"Owww," Cole whispered, rubbing his shoulder gingerly. "What was *that* for?"

"That's what Foreman's gonna do to Ali. And for Dixon's class. And for general principles. So we're on for five bucks?"

Cole sighed and lowered his arm. "Yeah."

Bobby and Cole crossed the street, entering the residential neighborhood of Rockwood.

"So, you goin' to Jason's party?" Bobby asked.

"You kiddin'? My dad wouldn't let me go in a million years."

"What're you talkin' about? You were at Conrad's party two weeks ago."

Cole picked up a small rock and tossed it at an oak tree in front of a brick ranch house.

"That's different," he said.

"Different? C'mon. I'm goin'. It'll be awesome. Why won't your dad let you go?"

"Dumbass. 'Cause Jason's… you know."

"Black? He's one of our best friends."

"Talk to my dad about it."

"That's stupid. Bet your dad would let you go if Jason was Muslim."

"He ain't Muslim. If Jason was Muslim, his name would be Yusef, or Ahmad, or somethin'."

"Whatever. So if Jason's name was Yusef, you'd be going to his party."

"Well… Hey, think they're playin' ball in the park?"

Bobby laughed. "I dunno, Cole. Might be some blacks there, though. Mister Prejudiced."

"Shut up, wiseass. There ain't never any blacks in our park. They play in their own park."

"Their own park? Where's that?"

"Dumbass. Where the politicians put the blacks. Dumbass."

Bobby stopped walking. "What? You don't know jack. Where they put 'em is they put 'em at the end of our park. So Rockwood Park is their park too, Mister Prejudiced."

Cole stopped a few feet ahead of Bobby and turned. "Stop *callin'* me that. *Where?*"

"The other side of the crawdad creek."

"No way!" Cole retorted. "The crawdad creek goes near the blacks?"

Bobby smiled. "Yep."

"The politicians would never put the blacks near the craw-dad creek."

"You're stupid. Why not?"

"'Cause— 'cause they can't swim."

Bobby rolled his eyes skyward. "Sometimes I can't even believe you're my best friend."

Both boys looked ahead at the entrance to Rockwood Park and its huge yawning opening beneath a canopy of overhanging oaks. The sun drenched the green grass for about thirty yards before the permanent shade and the sparse ground dictated by the ancient imperious trees.

"Race ya!" Cole declared, taking off in a sprint. "Five bucks!" he called over his shoulder.

The two boys ran down the sidewalk and into the park, its old-growth forest escorting them down the narrowing grassy lane. When they reached a bend, they pulled up, hands on knees.

"Pay up, slowpoke," Cole said, huffing.

"No way," Bobby said through his own heaving chest. "You cheated. Again."

"Waaah. Okay, crybaby. You don't gotta pay."

The boys took a look at the cavernous park ahead.

"Crap," Bobby said. "Nobody's here. Figures. The one day we don't have a football, nobody's playin'."

"Yeah," Cole agreed. "Murray's Law."

"You're stupid. *Murphy's* Law. Dumbass."

"How do *you* know? Murray coulda made the law. It could be Murray."

"Wanna bet? Five bucks." Bobby stuck out his right hand, the universal signal among boys in Durham, North Carolina that said 'I know I'm going to win.'

"Naw. It's not important like sports or nothin'. So whatcha wanna do? Gilligan's not on till four."

"Bet I can throw farther than you," Bobby said. Again he extended his right hand.

Again Cole rejected the handshake. "In your mama's dreams," Cole replied. "We don't have a ball, or I'd kick your butt."

"I know what. We both take a stick we wanna throw. Whoever throws farthest, wins."

"How much?" asked Cole.

"A slushee," said Bobby.

"One throw? For a slushee? I might not be warmed up."

"Waaaa. Okay. Fewest to the end of the park wins. Sorta like golf. And no excuses."

"'Kay," Cole confirmed. "But I'm Carolina and you're Duke."

"But," Bobby objected, "if it's like golf, we should be Nicklaus and Watson."

"Yeah, but that's namby-pamby. Besides, we're throwin', like Carolina and Duke. And I'm Carolina."

"I don't ever wanna be Carolina anyway. I'm Duke for sure. I call we play at Wallace Wade."

"But Kenan's nicer," Cole said.

"I called Wade first. We're playin' in Wade, or it's Nicklaus and Watson and you're Watson."

"'Kay. Selfish pig."

The boys carefully selected their sticks from the ample supply at the edge of the woods to their right. They measured their selections by holding them up side by side.

"No fair!" Bobby exclaimed. "Yours is bigger."

"Your mama tell you that?"

"That's *gross*."

"That's what your mama said."

"You don't know anything. Dumbass."

"Oh yeah?" Cole challenged Bobby. "I know Stephanie Moyer lives over that way," he said, pointing back the way they came.

Bobby picked up a rock and hit it with his stick, sending it ground-ball style into the thinning grass. "So?"

"So. I had a piece of that."

"No way. Stephanie hates you. You lie. When?"

"Um… summer. You were on vacation."

"Yeah? You lie. What base did you get to?"

"Um. Between first and second. 'Bout midway."

"Bullshit," Bobby replied. "You either got to first or you got to second. There's no midway in between. Which is it?"

"Lots of guys get between first and second."

"You mean they get thrown out is what they get. Stephanie Moyer threw you out. So you only got to first, not midway in between. That's so stupid."

Cole's face flushed red. "You don't know about it, 'cause you've never even made it to first. Dumbass."

Bobby's face developed its own tinge of color. "I don't want any Stephanie Moyer's tongue in my mouth anyway."

"*What?* That's not first!"

"Oh yeah? What's first then?"

"Well," Cole said. "If you don't know, why should I tell you?"

The boys continued to wander deeper into the park, taking turns hitting acorns with their sticks baseball-style.

"I know," Bobby said. "It's called a French kiss. You didn't know what a French kiss was. So you didn't get to any old first base with Stephanie Moyer."

"Yeah, but we just skipped right over it on the way to second," Cole offered confidently. "Stephanie wanted me to skip first, 'cause that's gross."

Bobby stopped again in his tracks. "So you skipped first but didn't get to second. So you didn't do anything at all with Stephanie Moyer. Loser. That means you and Stephanie just sat there!"

"We did lotsa stuff. You wouldn't understand the stuff between first and second, 'cause you're younger. The reason I didn't get to second is 'cause I stopped. I don't even like Stephanie."

"Stopped *what?*" Bobby was incredulous.

"Stopped doin' what you wouldn't understand, 'cause you're younger. *God*, I told you that already."

"Geez," Bobby said. "A whole three months. Three months isn't younger. Dumbass. Okay, so why were you between first and second with Stephanie Moyer if you don't even like her?"

"Man, are you stupid. Guys are *suppose* to make out with girls. You don't have to like 'em. James Bond knows that, and he makes out the most. See, he's always ready when the girl he's makin' out with tries to kill him. If James Bond liked 'em, he wouldn't be ready, 'cause he'd think they were really nice and all, and they'd kill him. We're *suppose* to make out. Likin' 'em's for Sunday school."

Bobby lowered his stick and then resumed walking. "Yeah, but I saw Goldfinger on TV, and James Bond was really mad at Goldfinger for killin' this girl James Bond liked. James Bond made out with her, and then Goldfinger killed her with a bunch of gold paint, and then James Bond went and killed Goldfinger 'cause James Bond actually wanted to marry that girl. They even called her Jill instead of Pussy, 'cause James Bond really liked her, and not just for makin' out and stuff."

"But that was so funny when that one girl's name was Pussy Galore," Cole said, giggling.

"Dumbass," Bobby retorted. "It was *supposed* to be funny. 'Cause the one he really liked was Jill, and that wasn't funny."

"Yeah, but he made out with Pussy Galore in a haystack in that barn, so he liked Pussy too."

Bobby stared at Cole for several seconds.

"Dumbass. He only made out with Pussy 'cause he wanted her to help him beat Goldfinger. Dumbass."

"Ha!" Cole laughed. "See what I mean? Gotcha. Likin 'em's for Sunday school. You just proved it. Ha!"

"Yeah, but… see… Jill was the one he… oh, forget it. Let's throw. Slushee, remember."

Bobby pointed ahead. "Let's throw this way. If we take this path it'll take us to the end of the park."

"I've never been down that way before," Cole said, barely above a whisper. "Is that… where the blacks live?"

"Yep. You throw first. I get last."

Cole stood and stared at the low canopy above the wide path. "I think my dad wanted me home soon."

"Your dad's still at work. If you're chicken, you should've said your mom. Throw or buy me a slushee."

Cole looked at his friend with resolve. "Ain't buyin' you no slushee."

Cole backed up a few paces, then readied for his toss.

"Here's Carolina, first and ten at the twenty!"

Cole ran forward for momentum, executed a crow hop, and heaved his stick, letting out a grunt. The stick spun through the air, a bit too high, striking a branch in the canopy of branches darkening their way.

"Not bad, but Duke tackles the Carolina receiver easily," Bobby narrated, extending the last three syllables for effect. He dropped back like a quarterback and threw his stick with equally prodigious effort. "First down Blue Devils at the fifty!" he proclaimed, thrusting his left arm forward like a referee advancing the chains.

Ten minutes later, the boys emerged from the trail and into bright sunlight. They picked up their sticks, Bobby's having edged Cole's by ten feet or so.

"What's that?" Cole asked, pointing his stick at what looked like the rear side of a two-story apartment complex. Several small buildings were strung together, with tricycles and two full clotheslines decorating a rear common area bordered on the park side by two blue Dempsey dumpsters.

"Told you that's where," Bobby said.

"You were right. There's the crawdad creek," Cole whispered, as if on a spy mission.

The boys approached the creek, which spanned about ten feet from bank to bank, providing a natural border between Rockwood Park and the apartment complex.

"They call this the projects, don't they?" Cole whispered again.

"Why are you whispering? Dumbass. Yes, they call this the projects. So what?"

"Do Muslims live there too?"

Bobby turned to face Cole. "I swear I don't know what's wrong with you. Let's go get my slushee."

"Okay. Hey! Double or nothin' I can hit that dumpster!"

Cole bent down and picked up a fist-sized rock from the creek bank. He pointed at the nearest of the two rusty, battered dumpsters.

"Don't *throw* that!" Bobby hissed.

"Why not? We're not on their property."

"Come on, dumbass. They might hear it."

"So? What're they gonna do? We'll just stay on our side of the creek."

"Cole. They might think you're throwin' at their *house*."

"Who cares? Their house sucks," Cole whispered, and pulled back his arm to throw the rock.

"Don't!"

Bobby winced as Cole hurled the rock, which clanged loudly against the side of the metal dumpster.

"Yes!" Cole exclaimed. "See if you can hit it."

"God, man," Bobby said in his turn to whisper. "That was stupid. You know people in there heard that. Maybe even saw it. It's their *house*. Dumbass."

"We ain't throwin' at their house. We're throwin' at their trash."

"Like you want them throwin' at *your* trash?"

"Shut up," Cole countered. "They're probly not even home. Come on out and play, ya Muslims!" he said without yelling.

Bobby stared at Cole in horror. "*Stop* that! Are you *crazy*?"

"See? Nobody's home."

As Cole delivered that last syllable, a door flew open. Five black teenage boys, ranging in age from early to late, emerged at a full sprint toward the creek.

"Oh, *crap!*" Cole and Bobby whispered in unison. They froze momentarily, until the realization arrived that the black boys were not going to stop. Cole and Bobby turned and ran toward the path into the park. When they reached the path, they pivoted to look, hope prominent on their faces.

"They won't cross the creek," Cole said. "They'd ruin their shoes."

They watched in horror as the biggest of the five jumped across the creek without slowing down. The others followed him with equal ease, landing on the bank to join their waiting leader.

Cole and Bobby wheeled and sprinted down the path into the shady dark of the park.

"They can't come into our park!" Cole hissed as they ran.

"They just did! I don't think it's our park, dumbass!" Bobby yelled from Cole's right as they plunged further toward home.

Bobby was sure he had never run this fast in his life, even when he'd approached the line of scrimmage as middle school quarterback and seen no linebacker positioned in the middle of the defensive side for Summit School and took a quarterback sneak seventy yards for a touchdown. This run would have to be longer, he knew. At least a hundred yards longer. Cole lagged ten feet behind him as Bobby risked a look back. The black boys were gaining on them. They meant business.

"They're gonna get us!" Cole screamed.

"Shut up and *run!*"

"Oh God oh God oh God oh God-God-*God* they're gonna kill us!"

Bobby slowed down just enough for Cole to catch up with him as they passed the bend that delivered them to their side of the park. Their pursuers were only ten yards behind, the biggest teen in the lead, followed by the other four at varying distances. Bobby couldn't afford to look back again.

They reached the embankment that led up a steep bare slope

populated by exposed tree roots that had always provided perfect footholds. Cole and Bobby scrambled up the slope, but Cole's left foot slipped off a root and he began sliding downward, screaming for Bobby to help. Bobby descended a couple of footholds, grabbed Cole, and pushed him back toward the top, but the delay was costly. As Cole pulled himself onto the ground above that bordered Garrett Avenue, a strong hand gripped Bobby's left ankle and pulled. Bobby struggled against the combined power of strength and gravity, and lost. He was dragged over the bumpy embankment's roots and deposited onto his back on the flat ground below, the wind knocked out of him by the force of the landing.

Wheezing from the pain and gasping for breath, Bobby looked up at the five looming faces. One, the oldest and biggest, reached down and grabbed Bobby's blue shirt collar.

"Come on, Marcus!" yelled one of the boys, a slightly portly kid of about fifteen. "Let's kick this white boy's ass!"

Marcus kept his eyes on Bobby's. "Shut up, Wayne," he said, his voice deep and controlled.

"But this boy's askin' for it. C'mon, man. Let's mess him up. Teach him a lesson!"

Marcus still didn't remove his focus from Bobby's eyes. Bobby didn't avert his own.

"Wayne, shut your mouth. Now listen, boy. What the hell were you doin', throwin' rocks at our house?"

Bobby's wind had recovered just enough to answer. "Man, I'm sorry. We were just playin'. We—"

"*Playin'*? So you think we're playin' with you now, boy?"

"No," Bobby whispered. "Definitely not."

"Damn right." Marcus looked up the embankment. "Where's your friend?"

"I dunno. Bringin' help, probly."

"He left you here."

"Um… no, he's gettin' help, I think. You—you should pro-bly go home."

Bobby didn't think that Marcus wanted to go home. He was right.

"He left you here, boy. Is he the one that threw the rock?"

"Who *cares*, Marcus? Two white boys come to our house and throw a rock, they gonna get hurt," Wayne said, objecting to Marcus's line of questioning.

Marcus ignored Wayne, his eyes searching Bobby's for something. Bobby tried desperately to think of what it was.

"You owe us somethin', boy. For disrespectin' our house."

"He owes us his ass in a sling, Marcus! We're gonna mess you *up*, white boy. Cut you good. Ain't we, Marcus? Teach this white boy about leavin' his white boy house."

Marcus turned to face Wayne. "You guys been watchin' too many movies." He turned back to Bobby. "Get up, boy."

Bobby struggled to his feet.

"Boy, what you owe us is—"

"A hundred bucks!" Wayne interjected. "Wanna come to our house, you gotta buy a ticket!"

"Wayne, say one more word, and I'm gonna let this white boy kick your ass."

Bobby closed his eyes for two seconds, then opened them. He didn't want to fight. Fortunately, neither did Wayne. Every-one stood in silence, until Marcus spoke again.

"Boy, what you owe us is an apology."

"An—an apology?" Bobby was stunned.

"An apology. What you think, we don't care if you come and shit on our house? How'd you like it if we came and threw rocks at your Labrador retriever or your mommy's station wag-on or some shit like that?"

"But—but I didn't shit on your house. My friend did."

Marcus stuck his right forefinger in Bobby's chest. "When

your friend shits on other people's houses and you got nothin' to say, you shit on other people's houses too. Boy."

Bobby looked around at the other faces. There was no sympathy here. Marcus was in charge, and Bobby figured he should be glad about that. If Wayne were in charge—

"Marcus, why can't we just teach this white boy a lesson?"

This time Wayne was less emotional in his suggestion. That scared Bobby more than Wayne's previous frenzy. It sounded… reasonable.

Marcus withdrew his finger from Bobby's chest and pushed it into Wayne's. "Wayne, you ever heard a white man apologize for shittin' on black people?"

Wayne shuffled his right foot in the dirt at the base of the embankment. "No."

"You ever heard a white *boy* do it? Even though it's their mommies and daddies and ancestors who've done most of the shittin'?"

"Um. No. But maybe just a black eye or somethin'. C'mon, Marcus. Like you said, he shit on our house."

"Wayne, if this white boy apologizes for what another white boy did, and apologizes for lettin' him do it, that's better than hurtin' his face."

In the silence that followed, Bobby wondered whether or not Marcus had ever hurt a white kid for shitting on his house, or maybe for shitting on somebody he cared about.

"I'm sorry we shit on your house," Bobby blurted, the words coming out in rapid fire. "I promise—"

"Stop right there, boy," Marcus said. "Anything else you say right now is bullshit. Until it isn't. Know what I mean?"

"Yes. I think so."

"Good." Marcus extended his right hand. Bobby took it. The handshake was firm.

"Where you goin' now, boy?"

"I guess to find my friend. Can you—can you stop callin' me 'boy'? My dad says that's racist."

Bobby heard a couple of the other kids gasp. Apparently it was rare that Marcus was challenged very seriously.

"Well," Marcus said. "That's interesting. I think it was Michelangelo who said he was still learning. Guess we should be too. What's your name?"

"I'm Bobby."

Marcus looked at his friends. "Bros, this is Bobby. Bobby, this is Wayne and Freddy and Malik and Terrance. Terrance, what your watch say?"

"Quarter to four," Terrance said. "Almost time to get back."

Marcus turned back to Bobby. "You watch Gilligan, Bobby?"

"Um, yes. When I don't have sports."

"Us too, dude. Wanna watch with us?"

Bobby was puzzled. He looked up the embankment for any sign of Cole. "With you? Where?"

"Our house. We got lots of Fritos and Pepsi too."

"Wait!" Wayne interrupted. "Ask him."

"Ask him what, Wayne?" Marcus asked.

"Ginger or Mary Ann?"

Everyone laughed, including Bobby, but all eyes focused on him. The question was real.

"Mary Ann," Bobby said, and held his breath.

"Bullshit," Wayne said. "I like that Ginger."

"Wayne, you so messed up," Terrance piped in. "You'd be makin' it with a buncha makeup. Mary Ann's where it's at."

The boys started walking back into the park, away from the embankment. Bobby hesitated, then fell in step.

"Here's my question, guys!" Bobby offered, hoping he wouldn't be dismissed.

All the boys stopped long enough to hear Bobby's question. "Ali or Foreman?"

With that, the debate raged back and forth, this way and that, as six boys walked together through the dark forest toward a television set across the crawdad creek. Bets were made, arguments were refuted, and Terrance won a stick-throwing contest, dethroning Marcus, before everyone got one shot at shooting their stick into the Dempsey dumpster.

SPIN THE BOTTLE

"Mrs. Singletary?"

"Yes?"

"Jane Singletary?"

"Um. Yes."

"John Hudson. Class of '97."

"John Hudson... John Hudson... from Milwaukee?"

"That's where we went to school together. St. Paul's. Class of '97. How've you been?"

"Great, John. Wow. It's... been a long time."

"Don't I know it. Too long."

"Do you shop here often? You—you live in St. Louis, John?"

"I don't. And I don't. Let's cut the small talk."

"Cut the... okay. Really, I was just looking at the cantaloupe. You approached me. And I'm glad for that. Really. I haven't seen a classmate since our fifteenth reunion. I—"

"Why did you kiss me, Jane?"

"Excuse me?"

"You heard me. Why did you kiss me?"

"Are you—are you talking about Homecoming? John, that was a long time ago. We were... we were just kids. And I think you kissed *me*, John. Not the other way around."

"Wait, Jane. Stop. Please don't hurry like that. I didn't mean to be so abrupt. Just turn around for a second. It's just that I've been wondering what I did wrong that night. Wait! Here, let me help you with that."

"Oh. Thank you. We have… two big dogs. Eating us out of house and home. As they say."

"We? Are you married, Jane?"

"Yes. My husband's name is Bill."

"Your husband died two years ago. Did you re-marry?"

"Excuse me? How did you know my husband died?"

"Alumni magazine. Died during a burglary, I think it said? He really should've owned a gun. Why did you lie about being married, Jane?"

"Why did… because to be honest, I'm a little alarmed to see you, John. When did you…"

"Get out? Twenty-two months and four days ago. I was innocent, Jane."

"They were supposed to notify me."

"You weren't the victim."

"No. That was Wendy. I imagine they notified Wendy. She was still seeing a shrink last time I saw her. Couldn't sleep with her husband, that sort of thing. Excuse me. I have to go."

"I can help you to your car after you check out."

"You will do nothing of the kind. Now let me past. Please."

"Why did you kiss me, Jane?"

"Let me past, or I will scream."

"Answer me, Jane. Or I will ask you again in your house."

"Let me *PAST!*"

"We're just having a conversation. One that can be continued at your house later if you prefer. Or tomorrow. Or next week. Or when you are showering."

"I have small children!"

"I know. Alumni magazine. Madison and Jenny. They're in the car."

"They're—what car? They're at school."

"Bill checked them out."

"Bill is *dead*, you sick prick! Let me past."

"You never informed the school. Big public schools don't just know things, you know. Bill's still on the yellow emergency contact forms. I do my homework. Answer my question. Why did you kiss me?"

"The school would've asked to see Bill's driver's license."

"No problem. The burglar took it. Hey, they never caught him, did they? That sucks. Why did you kiss me?

"I asked you a question, Jane. Why did you kiss me? Why did you *make out with me?* No, no. If you say a word to the cashier, I swear they will never figure out which car trunk is mine. It's not like I parked in the lot. We did attend a quality school together, you know. Now stop looking around like I've done something to you. Just answer my question and we can go on to the next step."

"You killed my *husband?* But it was a burglary. The man wore a—"

"Okay! So I took the wallet. Guilty as charged. Answer my question."

"I kissed you because it was my first kiss. To get it out of the way."

"You made out with me to… get it out of the way. I see. Nice. Take your cart to the front and check out. I will go with you."

"Where are Madison and *Jenny*, you—"

"Now don't get frantic. I took them because it was my first kidnapping. To get it out of the way. Bill was also my first— *Stop that!* Hitting me in the face isn't going to fix anything. Want me to push the cart?

"Good. Now isn't that better for those flippity-floppity triceps than slapping an old classmate in the face? You're taking this all very personally, you know. It's not like your children are dead. Or are they?"

"Welcome to Kroger! Paper or plastic?"

"Plastic. Can I see a—"

"We don't need to see a manager, ma'am. Your cantaloupes were a bit green, and my wife's understandably upset. Our daughters enjoy cantaloupe. Here, Jane. Let me pay. My Citi card has plenty of room."

"It's twenty-nine sixteen, ma'am."

"Here's your receipt. Thanks for shopping at Kroger!"

"This way, Jane. Stop crying. We can go in my car. Stop— *stop* that. Let's just go home and let the kids play while we talk. Or we can go have a cocktail somewhere while they stay in the trunk. I'm sure there must be plenty of oxygen getting in. By the way, are they good nose-breathers?"

"If my husband were still alive, he would kill you."

"If your husband were still alive, you would not be. Your marriage was over either way."

"Where is your car?"

"It's about a mile away. No worries. You drive. I'll direct. There. Buckle up."

"Why are you doing this?"

"I told you. I need to know."

"Know *what*, you— I'm sorry. Please don't hurt my children."

"Go left here, then stay straight until you get to Tyler Avenue, then right. I need to know why you made out with me. It wasn't to get it out of the way. I saw you playing Spin the Bottle at Shawn Price's party freshman year, when his parents were on that ski trip. I'd say you certainly had gotten it out of the way well before that.

"Jane. Did you love me?"

"Did I *love* you? How can you ask me that? Of course not. We were kids. And why would it matter now if I had? Turn right here?"

"Yes. Then stay straight for a couple of miles."

"I thought you said your car was a mile away."

"My car is a rental. It's parked at the playground in the park near your house. I took an Uber to the grocery store after you left home. You sure took your time with that BLT. Anyway, a good guess on my part. You're as regular as clockwork. Wednesdays after lunch, off you go to the Kroger."

"But Madison and Jenny…"

"I imagine they're at recess. It's after lunch. Jenny sure loves those monkey bars."

"You mean—"

"I know you're relieved."

"Then where are we going?"

"How much did you get from the life insurance?"

"That's none of your business."

"Actually, I think it is. I think Madison and Jenny do too. They're counting on you today. To do the right thing."

"Five million. Invested in Vanguard through a trust. We live off the investment income."

"You certainly do."

"You can't touch that money because I can't either. It's in a family trust. The principal can't be touched until both girls graduate from college."

"Did I ask you for money, Jane? You insult me."

"Then why did you ask about the life insurance?"

"To see how profitable it was for me to do you the biggest favor of your life."

"You're sick. You're—"

"I changed my mind. Take the parkway exit. West."

"West? But why?"

"Just do it. Now."

"Why are we going out of the city? My kids get out of school in an hour."

"They can attend aftercare. Just like last Thursday when

you breezed in forty minutes late in your tennis outfit and Oakleys."

"That was pre-arranged and paid for. We do aftercare every Thursday."

"Well. Wednesday will have to do. You're going too fast. Slow down."

"No."

"You're trying to get us pulled over. You think I don't know what you're doing? Slow the hell down!"

"No."

"Madison and Jenny aren't at school, Jane."

"Yes, they are."

"No. They aren't. They're in the trunk of my rental. I was just testing your capacity for cooperation."

"Bullshit."

"Slow down *now*, goddammit! You're doing ninety!"

"That I am."

"You're going to get us pulled over, you bitch."

"If you don't like it, John, why don't you hop out?"

"Because Madison and Jenny aren't at school, Jane. And I confess that they aren't in the trunk of my rental."

"Oh, really, you bastard? Why don't I go a hundred, then?"

"Because they're in the back. Enjoying your Mario Andretti impression, I have to imagine… That's better. Drop it another ten."

"They're at *school*. My kids are at *school!*"

"They're in your trunk. Here. I took a picture…

"You should see your face. Yes, the gags are the socks from your nasty gym bag. Not from Thursday tennis, I pray. I'm sure they don't taste any better than they smell."

"I'm getting off at the next exit. You're suffocating them!"

"No. You're suffocating them, Jane. I'm not even here."

"You're not—"

"Exactly. I've never even been to St. Louis. I'm in Milwaukee, minding my own business, while you're being one of those crazy moms who murders her own kids. No wonder you never kissed me again. You have a cold, cold heart."

"I can get at the principal. I can withdraw ten percent of it in a calendar year. I'll give it to you. That's a half million dollars. Please. I love my children."

"I have money, Jane. My dad owned fifteen sub shops, remember? But I don't have love. Thanks to you."

"*Madison! Jenny!* Can you hear me? Mommy's here! You're gonna be okay!"

"Jane, did you know that some people have started saying LOL out loud, instead of actually laughing?"

"I'm getting off at this exit."

"Sounds good. You can drop me off at Sonic or something. Then I'll phone the police and give them your make, model and license plate number. After all, you have your kids tied up and gagged in the trunk. Good luck with that."

"The kids are old enough to tell the police about you. And the school can identify you."

"Jane. You didn't take your kids to school today."

"Of course I did."

"Let's drive to California. Leave it all behind. Pick up where we left off with that kiss."

"You mean, like a re-do?"

"Sure. But it's do-over. Not re-do. You *re-do* your hair. You *do-over* your life."

"So you're telling me to keep driving west. You promise not to hurt my kids?"

"You have my word of honor, Jane. If you promise to kiss me every day for the rest of your life."

"Can I put on the cruise control?"

"Yes. Or do you want a Big Mac? You could check on the kids when we're sitting in the drive-through."

"I could do that. Maybe they're getting hungry."

"You could ask them."

"No. They would insist on apple juice."

"You're a good mother."

"Thank you. I was a good wife too."

"Indeed you were, my darling. And a damned good kisser."

"You know how I got ready for that Spin the Bottle game at Shawn Price's house, John?"

"No. But I have a feeling you're going to tell me."

"LOL. I kissed the mirror in their half bath."

"That's very, um, inventive."

"It only works if you turn your head sideways."

"Cool. Where did you learn that?"

"That's easy, John. I learned it from you."

"Those are blue lights back there. Check your mirror."

"Yes, they are."

"They must've clocked you a mile back. You were pushing a hundred. Bitch. Stop on the shoulder and let me out."

"I will do no such thing."

"Do it, god damn it!"

"I got you, John."

"Let me *OUT*!"

"I wouldn't kiss you again with a gun to my head."

"You would for your **KIDS**! *Let me out of the goddamn car!*"

"They've got you now, John. LOL. They'll find my kids. Like the man said, you son of a bitch... don't bend over for the soap."

"I think you've done enough to me, Jane. Why don't you just let me out? You have to stop anyway. Why take both of us down? Let me out and I'll run. Then you can blame me. It's perfect."

"Too late now, John. I'm already stopped. The officer's getting out of his car."

"I can see that, Jane. Turn off the child locks, please."

"Not until the officer checks the trunk and puts you in cuffs, you monster."

"Cop looks kind of ticked, Jane. Roll down your window. Before he breaks it."

"Officer, thank God you're here!"

"Ma'am, there's an amber alert out for this vehicle."

"I thought so! The trunk! Hurry!"

"I'm sorry, but I'm going to need you to step out of the car. You were evading active pursuit. First I need your license and registration."

"No problem… Here you go. Why aren't you looking in the *trunk?* Get him before—"

"What's in the bag, ma'am?"

"The bag? Why aren't you looking in the **TRUNK**? He said he put them in the—"

"We're going to need to look in the bag, ma'am. Step aside."

"The trunk… my babies."

"Step away from the car door, ma'am."

"Are you looking for my babies? God bless you if you're looking for my babies."

"Yes, Mrs. Hudson. We're looking for your babies."

THE ENVELOPE

✳ ✳ ✳

The black manila envelope with stark white letters popping from the gloss leaned casually against the lazy susan, as if it had all day. And it did. The officers outside arrived less than fifteen minutes after the certified mail, for which Jeremiah refused to sign before it was signed for him with a shrug by the delivering deputy.

"What about the back door?"

The hope in his wife's voice made it worse.

"You know they're back there, Elizabeth."

"Do they want Terrance too?" Dread and hope, ten seconds apart.

"He's fifteen. Can't be conscripted for another year."

Jeremiah rose and placed another blueberry coffee in the Keurig. Putting his old Black Lives Matter mug under the dispenser, he pushed the button for the largest cup size, grabbed the spoon and three Splenda packets from the counter, and returned to the breakfast nook.

"It was just a matter of time, Elizabeth. I've had a good life."

Elizabeth slapped her right palm on the round oak table. "You're forty-one, baby. Stop talking like that. It took two years to get the envelope. Most of the conscripted are in their teens and twenties. Some in their thirties. What do they need *you* for?"

"Elizabeth, you got to understand. They're running low on the most productive brothers. They were gonna start with over-forties soon enough. I talk like this because it's inevitable. But now that it's happened, I need you to take Terrance and Jolene and get to Canada. That's what Cadence did with their kids when Robert was conscripted. Remember?"

"How do you know they made it? We haven't had cell phones or computers for so long, and when they stopped mail delivery to brown folks' homes we shoulda known. If you leave the country, you really leave the country. No saying hi to no-body." She paused. "Open the envelope. Maybe it'll say where you're going."

"Labor conscription doesn't work that way, baby. It's not like you can come visit."

"How long do they wait before they come in to get you?"

"I don't know." Jeremiah returned to the Keurig and re-trieved his mug. Sitting back down, he tore the Splenda packets after giving their bottoms three taps, then poured and stirred. The clank of the spoon echoed throughout the kitchen.

"I'm going to get Terrance up," Elizabeth said. "Jolene too."

Jeremiah held up his left palm, as if to stop traffic as he sipped his coffee. Setting the mug on the table, he whispered, "I don't want them to remember watching their daddy go off to be a slave."

His wife brought her palms to her face, tears welling. Im-mediately Jeremiah regretted his choice of words.

"I know, Elizabeth. I'll get paid. A buck above minimum wage. Those old white men think of everything. No Thirteenth Amendment as long as you get a W-2. It's just the labor draft. Best for the economy and all that. I'm just unlucky to be brown is all. So's Jose Ramirez over on Autumn Grace. He got the en-velope on Tuesday, so's I hear. Tom Jansen told me when we were both putting out the trash. Bastard had a big old smile on his face. Motherf—"

"Jeremiah!"

"I'm being quiet. Glad you agree about letting the kids sleep."

Jeremiah examined his mug. "I hear they call them dormitories."

"What? Where you'll live?"

"Yeah. But I think it's those tent cities they built for immigrant kids back in the orange man's first term. This is what they had in mind."

"How long before they get tired of waiting? Do they use warrants?"

"For labor conscription the envelope is the warrant."

"I think you should open it. All you know is what you've heard. Maybe it's, like, a year or something. Like… a deployment."

Jeremiah looked at his wife. "Yeah. When was the last time you saw Royce Phillips?"

Elizabeth stared past Jeremiah. "About… a year and a half ago."

"And Tamera?"

Silence rang in Jeremiah's ears. When his wife spoke, she whispered.

"They don't take mothers."

"How do you know that? The Phillips kids weren't all out of the nest when Royce got the envelope."

"The girl was sixteen."

A chill shimmied along Jeremiah's arms. "You know what that means, Elizabeth. Tamera was conscripted for the seamstress shops in New Mexico. And the girl—"

"STOP IT!"

"You can't say it, can you? But you know it's coming. The pleasure hotels. That's where the Phillips girl is."

"But Jolene's only thirteen. Maybe—"

"Elizabeth. There's no maybe. The minute she turns sixteen, our baby girl's legal to be drafted for the pleasure industry. That's when you'll get the envelope to go to New Mexico. You'll all three get the envelope. Terrance first, in less than a year. Stop acting like it's just the fathers. That's dreaming, baby. Canada. You can't just wait."

Jeremiah stood and adjusted his belt to match the slight paunch in his middle. He started to extend his right hand to his wife's cheek, but stopped when a tear beat him to her supple brown skin.

"I got something I need to do," he said.

Jeremiah crossed from the kitchen to the open living room, then turned left when he reached the cased opening that led directly into the den. He pulled the left side of his desk away from the wall. Lifting the mauve carpet hard enough to pull the tacks from the plywood underflooring, he opened the small hinged door he'd installed when the news came that the Supreme Court had upheld the president's executive order to withhold Second Amendment protections for all minorities of color. He withdrew the Walther PPX revolver from its two-year residence beneath his desk. He stroked the barrel three times, then set it down on his desk and lift-thumped the cherry piece back into place.

Picking up the gun, he advanced to the den window, which faced the tree line on the west side of the house. He pulled the embroidered curtain back just enough to peer out. Sure enough, there were two men posted there, weapons drawn to the ready. There would be no escape in any direction, even with the Walther. He retreated from the window and sank into his high-backed black leather swivel chair.

Closing his eyes, Jeremiah remembered the time he first saw the old televised debate in London between James Baldwin and William F. Buckley. He'd listened to Baldwin with a mix of horror and relief; horror at the centuries of black suffering in America, relief that most of it was behind him, behind his children. The quaintness of such relief was now impossibly distant, a speck of memory, like trying to remember what cotton candy tasted like when he was six. The journey of the black person in America was circular, in a Lovecraftian kind of way. His mother had always told him he was living in the second half of a V. "The low part, Jeremiah, but it's moving up and there ain't no gravity that's going to stop it," she'd loved to say. But sitting here now, he knew he'd always lived in a circle with no exit, except for the one now resting in his right hand.

He could survive slavery. His ancestors had. Of course, they'd had no choice. It was legal. So was the labor draft. And now here he was, living in the downward curve of the white circle, the light above diminishing with the growing distance as he realized that for him, and for his wife and children, the circle would not travel its upward curve. It would not produce its Lincoln. Today the circle would become the last line in an M.

"And then will come a period," he whispered, rising to climb the stairs to visit his sleeping children for the very last time.

SURE VINE

The email was brief. Except for its content, Travis Schamades would have been prepared to relegate the message to the spam heap. It was "personal", addressed to Travis by name, and the "From" said the sender was Sure Vine. Sounded like the vendor was in the wine business, and maybe the wine shop sold its damned customer list *again*.

But the wine shop had not sold its customer list again, or perhaps they had but who cares. This was one weird message. Travis read it six times before forwarding it to the Bureau and to Marnie Taft over at Homeland Security.

Coffee was ready in the kitchen. Travis continued to stare at the message, wondering how long it would take for Marnie's boys to run this nutcake down.

The sender had chosen a blue font color, size 12, all italic. Before getting his morning coffee, Travis read the words one more time, though he was pretty sure he had them memorized by now. Such an odd little message:

Dear Travis,

My name is Sure. I say this to you because I consider it as silly to call me God as it would be to call your dog 'Dog' instead of 'Sheba'. Anyway, it's time to cut it out. Seriously. It's just getting to be that time. So Travis , and all the rest of you, cut it out. Now.

All the best,
Sure Vine

The landline rang just as Travis rose to retrieve his coffee. He considered whether he could get the coffee and still answer by the fourth ring, and calculated in the negative. Annoyed, he sat back down at his desk and picked up the charcoal receiver.

"Travis Schamades."

"Travis," said the voice.

"Marnie," said Travis.

"What's your dog's name?" said the voice.

"Sheba," said Travis.

"We've got a problem, Travis."

"That's what I was thinking."

"Travis?"

"Yeah."

"I have a cat."

"I thought you had a pot-bellied pig."

"Shut up. I have a cat."

"That's cool."

"Travis."

"Yes."

"My cat's name is Caesar."

"That's very interesting."

"Sure Vine told me to cut it out, too. Only he said it would be really silly to call my cat 'Cat' instead of Caesar."

"Jesus. Someone's been doing their homework."

"Travis."

"Yes."

"Turn on CNN."

"We have a problem?"

"A doozy."

"I'll call you back," said Travis.

Travis went into the TV room and picked up the remote from the coffee table. He turned on CNN and stood in front of the television. The announcer, an attractive brunette dressed appropriately for a soiree at, let's see, 9:19 a.m., looked mildly amused as she read the words from the teleprompter.

"...apparently appeared on computers and phones worldwide at 7:07 Eastern Daylight Time. Again, preliminary investigation reveals that the message appears to have been altered or personalized for each email address, potentially all email addresses in the world, something which computer experts had considered impossible until the past hour or so. High school alma maters, advanced degrees, pets' names, et cetera have been identified in the messages, suggesting by far the largest breakdown in online security in the history of the Internet. The hacker responsible for the crime has identified himself as 'Sure Vine', which analysts here at CNN believe to be an English anagram for 'Universe'. In a variety of languages across the globe, the hacker now known as Sure Vine has told each reader to, in American vernacular, 'cut it out'."

Travis Schamades's knees wobbled a bit as he sank into the gray leather sofa in the TV room. A doozy all right, he thought, and he called Marnie back.

"Marnie Taft," said the voice.

"A doozy all right," said Travis.

"Travis," said the voice.

"Yes."

"This is the real deal. Isn't it."

"I think it's the real deal."

"I think it's the real deal too."

"That's what you said. I just agreed with you."

"I know, Travis. What do we do now?"

"I dunno. I'm just a Bureau analyst. You're Homeland Security."

"I didn't think God was on the list," said Marnie.

"You mean Sure."

"Sorry," said Marnie.

"No problem," said Travis.

"What do you think the Industry's going to do?"

"Well," said Travis, "if it's the real deal..."

"Sure?"

"Sure. If Sure's the real deal, the Industry's going to have to make sure Sure's the Devil."

"That's a thought. Just the Devil impersonating Sure."

"Sounds like the smartest thing."

"Travis."

"Yes."

"Why would the Devil tell everybody to cut it out?"

"Because that's what Sure would say."

"Brilliant. Think the Industry's on it already?"

"They're highly capable folks. By lunch is my best guess. They'll get it handled. Then the Pope'll do a heck of a job condemning the hacker, and we can get back to business as soon as the President says it's okay."

"Travis?"

"Yes, Marnie."

"Thank you. You're a hell of an analyst."

"Thanks. It was a doozy, though."

"I'll take it to the Secretary. He's got a red line to the Industry."

"Oh, damn," said Travis.

"Problem?" said Marnie.

"I'm out of Equal," said Travis.

"Drink it black. It won't kill you."

"Sure. Have a good one."

"Right back at you."

ODE TO CUBBY

❋ ❋ ❋

She placed the bear on the tenth step from the bottom. He was an old bear, well-used or well-loved, or maybe both. He had a sky-blue ribbon attached to his head, but not by the manufacturer. Oh no, Stephen thought, certainly not by the manufacturer. *That* ribbon was put on *that* bear by a child. Now, as the bear posed for a photograph less than a hundred feet from Abraham Lincoln, perhaps thirty fewer from the memory of Martin Luther King, Jr. and his dream, the woman was ready.

She was black, older than thirty but less than forty, and the sort of next-door pretty that had always made Stephen want to become a dad. Her complexion was like a tan cream, smooth and supple like Alicia Keyes or Marilyn McCoo of the Fifth Dimension. Curved lines bordered the outsides of her eyes, lines that suggested lots of laughter or lots of worry, or maybe both. From her neck hung a camera, the bigger kind that made Stephen think of old Nikon commercials he'd seen on YouTube.

The woman employed her empty left hand to brush wavy dark-brown hair from her eyes, then smiled and said something to the bear. Stephen couldn't hear her words from his seat at the top of the steps, but he could tell they were reassuring, calming. She was telling the bear that this would be a special photograph. Then she was listening, nodding her head in agreement.

Suddenly the bear said something important, something that mattered a great deal to the woman. Her eyes changed. Surprised, she brought the palm of her left hand to her open mouth, covering it, saddened or even appalled by the bear's words. With her right hand she raised the camera, but lacked the strength to hold it steady without the reinforcement that could be offered by the hand that stifled her emotion. Stephen almost jumped to his feet to offer assistance, but held back as the woman wiped a tear from her left eye with her empty hand, then lent the hand to the camera, steadying it in partnership with the right. She examined the viewfinder, then took the picture. Then another. Then she repositioned the bear, turning him to face Lincoln. She moved to her right so that she could capture the bear in profile, gazing at Lincoln, Lincoln gazing at him, an unspoken mutual love that seemed to say they got each other.

Stephen wanted to be in this photograph. He wanted the picture to live in this woman's house, and he wanted to be in it, to live in her house by being in the picture. But he couldn't ask a stranger to include him in a family photo. Part of him, however, suggested that maybe this wasn't a family photo. Maybe the woman was getting to be an old maid of sorts, and brought her childhood bear to Washington, DC for cute pictures she could share on Facebook with her other single friends as they navigated their lonely lives in the false company of social media. Or maybe...

Stephen stopped. Not this woman. She wasn't pathetic. She wasn't deluded. This wasn't her bear. This was her child's bear. So where was her child? The bear wanted to know.

So did Stephen. Why would a woman take pictures of her child's bear in front of the Lincoln Memorial? Why would she reassure the bear, an inanimate object that couldn't say anything back? At that moment Stephen decided he needed to know the answer.

The woman scooped up the bear and carried him down the steps, his bottom resting on her right forearm, his head against her right chest. She was careful with each step, patiently descending while keeping the ride smooth, not wanting to jar the bear before arriving back at the stroller that awaited their return.

That's it! Stephen thought. Sure. The bear belonged to a baby or toddler whose sleep wasn't worth interrupting for a photo at the Lincoln Memorial. After all, she'd only been ten steps away, and got the photos she wanted without going too far from the child in the stroller. Stephen was relieved. Still, he wanted a look at the child. He or she had a wonderful mother, and years later would appreciate the mother's documentation not only of their trip to the nation's capital, but of the importance of the bear in their lives, and theirs in the bear's.

As the woman lowered the bear into the stroller, careful to cradle his head, Stephen descended the steps, looking back once at America's sixteenth president, and gave the stroller a wide-enough berth to avoid detection by the woman. Once they were both moving forward, he could fall in behind her, perhaps looking at his phone, and then speed up enough to see the child while passing by. Stephen held his phone up as if taking a video of the Memorial, but his eyes were on the woman and stroller who shared the iPhone screen with Father Abraham.

She finished settling the bear into the stroller, then stepped behind, gripped the handle with hands a foot apart, unlocked the stroller wheels with her right foot, and started her journey toward what Stephen assumed would be the next monument on her visit to Washington. Stephen wondered what the next destination would be, but didn't have to wait long for the answer, as the woman headed directly toward the reflecting pool. Stephen followed about fifteen feet behind. Even when he craned his neck, he couldn't see far enough into the stroller to see the sleeping toddler or baby who shared with the bear the comfort within.

He decided to pass her, just so he could see inside the stroller. Why would she take pictures of the child's bear but not the child? The question was driving him crazy. He had to see.

He drew even with the stroller, concealing his intent by looking at his raised phone. About six feet to the woman's left, he risked the glance that would answer his question. Girl or boy? Baby or toddler? Black or white? Mother or nanny?

Stephen saw into the stroller and immediately stopped walking. There was no child in the stroller. Only the bear, nestled among pillow pets that included a grinning Spongebob Squarepants and a dour Eeyore. The woman had tucked the bear in beneath a light blue blanket. Stephen had been right. The bear was a boy.

He wanted another look, perhaps even a chance to take a picture. Wait. Not one picture. Two. One of the bear with his friends Spongebob and Eeyore, and another of the woman. He resumed walking, at a swift pace so he could take the bear photo from behind and then to get far enough ahead to snap the photo he wanted most.

He'd seen the woman before. He was sure of it. It wasn't because she reminded him of Marilyn McCoo. He'd seen her before. Damn it, he *had*. But where?

He could ask her. He could take the pictures first. That was important. Get the pictures first, in case she didn't want to talk to him. And then he could ask her if she'd ever been to Charlotte. It had to have been Charlotte. Stephen had never been anywhere else before now. Tomorrow was the last day of the field trip to Washington, and then it was back to Charlotte for the rest of tenth grade. Back to the little house two blocks from Independence Boulevard behind the Wendy's, where from his bedroom he'd heard the Dempsey dumpsters being emptied twice a week on the other side of the big wooden fence that had been his view for as long as he could remember.

When he drew close enough, he put his phone camera on the Portrait setting and took three pictures of the bear. The first two were zoom-ins. For the third, Stephen included Spongebob and Eeyore, because all three of them looked like they weren't new. They'd been together for a long time, the three of them. Stephen envied them. They looked happy, even though their mother did not. At this point, Stephen realized two things: First, the bear and Spongebob and Eeyore were lucky. And second, Stephen loved their mother.

Stephen sped his pace to get far enough ahead to get her picture. It could go on his dresser. So could the bear and Spongebob and Eeyore. At least until his dad would see them and whip his behind again for not wanting to play football this year and adding insult to injury by taking pictures of stuffed animals in strollers and women who looked both beautiful and familiar.

When he figured he'd gotten ahead of the stroller by twenty feet or so, Stephen turned and focused his phone on the Lincoln Memorial, then lowered the phone to include the woman. Later he could enlarge the picture to include only her and the stroller. He took the picture, then two more for good measure. Better safe than sorry. He returned the phone to his right khaki pocket just as the woman and the stroller drew close to him and stopped.

"Did you just take a picture of me?" the woman asked. Her tone was unchallenging. Curious, even.

Embarrassed, Stephen lied. "No, ma'am," he said. "I took it of President Lincoln."

"Oh," the woman said. "Sorry." She looked disappointed.

"But I—I can take one of you and your... baby. If you like. I mean—"

"That's okay," said the woman, smiling. "I already took one."

"Yes, I, um, I saw you."

"You look familiar," the woman said, losing the smile but not in a bad way, her eyes locked on Stephen's.

Stephen considered telling the woman that she looked familiar too, but thought it would be too weird. He stood in awkward silence, trying hard to resist telling the woman that he loved her. That would be even weirder than saying she looked familiar to him too. If he actually said she looked familiar to him too, he was sure he would have to tell her he loved her, and in what world would that make sense? He didn't love her in the way he wanted Charisse in the junior class to love him, but he loved this woman nonetheless and certainly couldn't tell her that. So he told her nothing.

"I've seen you before," the woman said. "Do you live in Fairfax?"

Stephen was relieved to shift the conversation to geography.

"No, ma'am. I live in Charlotte, North Carolina. I'm on a field trip with my—"

"Charlotte!" the woman exclaimed. "Where in Charlotte? I grew up in Dilworth." Then she smiled the most beautiful smile Stephen had ever seen.

"Near Independence Boulevard by the Wendy's," Stephen said, then cursed himself. He should've lied, he told himself. If she grew up in Dilworth, she'd think better of him if he grew up in Myers Park. Too late.

"Well, there's more than one Wendy's on Independence Boulevard, but that's cool," she said. "So Charlotte must be where I've seen you before. Did you say you're on a field trip?"

"Yes. I go to East Mecklenburg."

"East Meck! Wow. I went to Myers Park High School. I was lucky. Though there weren't a lot of black people there then. Don't know about now."

"Yes, ma'am. I mean, no, there aren't a lot of black people at Myers Park. Sort of like at Country Day. My mom tried to get me in there, but my dad wouldn't let me go. He said they'd see me as a token."

The woman's expression changed. "You mean your dad thought you shouldn't have that kind of opportunity just because you're black? I'm… so sorry."

The woman looked sad.

"It's okay," Stephen said. "My dad doesn't like white people so much. Sometimes I think it's because he's not my real dad, and my real dad was white."

"Well," the woman said, the smile returning to her face. "You're a very handsome young man. So your real dad was white. So what? My dad was white too. I guess our dads were kind of alike. My dad was married to a black woman—my mom—but he didn't like it when *I* got married to a white man. No, sir, he didn't like that at all. My dad was a bit of a hypocrite, I got to tell you."

"I'm sorry, ma'am."

The woman stood in silence.

"Ma'am?" Stephen said.

"Oh! I'm sorry. Yes?"

"Why did you take a picture of the bear in front of the Lincoln Memorial?"

The woman lifted her gaze to the cloudy sky.

"I do that this day every year," she said, barely above a whisper. Her voice was hoarse, as if she was about to cry.

Stephen waited, then said "Every year," but more as a prompt to continue.

"Yes. It must've looked like I belonged in an asylum, right? Talking to the bear like he's my child?"

"No, ma'am. I liked it. That's um… that's why I followed you. I promise I'm not a stalker."

The woman laughed. "I know you're not. I take that picture every year because somewhere in the world, my boy is growing up, and I don't get to be there with him. So I, you know… I bring his bear and his bear's friends to a place I always wanted to bring my kid. I take a picture here, and another at the Martin Luther King monument. Pictures of a world that could've been for our country, in a life that could've been for me. As a mother, you see. This was my boy's bear when he was a baby. Sponge-bob and Eeyore too. They were his favorites."

"I'm so sorry, ma'am. Did he..."

"Oh no! He's not dead. No. He was only ten months old when my husband was deployed to Afghanistan. Fourteen years ago today. My husband was killed by a roadside bomb just six days after he got there. A road outside of Kabul. I was only twenty. My dad convinced my mom that I should give up my baby because I couldn't make enough money to raise him right, and they both worked about fifty hours a week. They wore me down until I gave in. I was just a kid, you see. I didn't know how much I'd—He was adopted. He—"

The woman began to cry. She put both hands to her face, as if embarrassed.

"I'm sorry, ma'am. I shouldn't have asked. I'm so sorry."

She shook her head, removing her hands from her wet face. "Don't be. I don't get to talk about it very often. My husband never wants to hear about my boy, wherever my boy is. I don't blame him. It just makes me sad, and he loves me. He doesn't want me to be sad, and he thinks not talking about my boy is the best way to deal with it. So thank you. I'm glad you followed me."

The woman stuck her hand out. Stephen shook it.

"I'm Madeleine," the woman said.

"I'm Stephen," Stephen said.

The woman named Madeleine looked at Stephen as if she'd been shot.

"Don't say that," she said.

"Don't say... what, ma'am?"

"Don't say your name is Stephen."

"Wh—what should I say?"

"Anything you want. Just not Stephen."

Stephen looked around at several passersby. Nobody was

curious about the interaction between him and the woman named Madeleine.

"Why? Was your son named Stephen?"

"Yes. And now you think you're my son. Don't you?"

"Ma'am, I don't know anything about anything. I only know that I love you. I don't know why. I can call myself Henry if you like."

"Henry," the woman said. "I like that name." She stepped closer and drew Stephen into an embrace. "I love you, Henry."

Stephen hugged the woman as hard as he could. As he did, he whispered, "Should I go to Country Day?"

"Yes," she whispered in his ear. "I'll pay for it."

Thirty seconds later, they ended their embrace. "You probably have a tour bus," the woman said. "Go. My last name is Francis. Madeleine Francis. Send me a friend request."

"As Stephen?" Stephen said a silent prayer.

Madeleine Francis looked at Stephen for more than ten seconds.

"Yes. As Stephen."

Stephen turned to make his way back to the Memorial and his tour group.

"Stephen!"

Stephen turned. "Yes, Mom?"

Madeleine Francis reached into the stroller. "Here," she said. She handed him the bear, but removed the ribbon first. "We called him Cubby. You even said the first syllable, a couple days before you left. It was the first word you tried to say."

"Cubby," Stephen said. "And Spongebob?"

"Get to know Cubby first, baby. We got all the time in the world. Oh, and Stephen?"

"Yes, Mom?"

"Let's take a selfie. In front of Father Abraham. Oh yeah, and Stephen?"

Stephen laughed. "Yes, Mom."

"Don't forget Cubby."

THE GLAD PROMISE

S he never looked at the camera. That much he remembered.

On the morning of his fortieth birthday, Crafton Kelly kept the promise he'd made twenty years ago. If Sandy wasn't married when she and Crafton were both forty, he would go to her. She had turned her page of the calendar two months ago. Now Crafton had arrived as well. She would be glad.

As he reviewed the photos on her Facebook page, Crafton marveled again at how young she still looked. Her full, kissable mouth remained both, so much so that he wanted to kiss the screen of his iPhone. He saw no evidence of crow's feet. The laugh lines forming rounded vees on her cheeks were beckoning assets. But the eyes. The eyes. They still never looked at the camera. On some photos, like the ones with old friends from college, all of them except Sandy grinning at the viewer while hamming it up at their fifteenth reunion three years ago, she matched their laughter. But her eyes gazed off into the distance, taking her somewhere else.

The eyes. The eyes were looking for him. Waiting for him. Longing for Crafton Kelly to turn forty and keep his promise.

Crafton was nothing if not a man of his word. She would be glad.

Facebook said she lived in Chattanooga. Sandra Triplett McKay. Worked at Wellington Ford, it said. Crafton wondered again why Facebook always said 'worked' for present-tense employment, but didn't dwell on the question. He needed to finish packing. The drive from Atlanta to Chattanooga would take two hours. Rush hour heading north on 75 on a Friday afternoon always added thirty minutes nowadays, especially when leaving from Marietta.

Her ruminations on loss last year, posted to Facebook, had been painful for Crafton to read. Maybe she just wanted to honor the dead by pretending to grieve. Don McKay had been a jackass throughout college. Leopards don't change their spots. Crafton had said this to himself often over the past eighteen years. Well, seventeen actually. That's how long it took for Sandy to be single again. Seventeen years of living with a jackass. No wonder she never looked at the camera.

She'd been looking for him.

As he finished packing his black leather duffel bag, Crafton again admired her patience. Like Crafton, she'd known that forty would one day arrive in all its exuberant joy. Don McKay's accident had merely released more sunshine through the approaching doorway to the resumption of happiness. And there were no children on her Facebook page. Bright sunshine.

Crafton slowly and silently zipped up the duffel bag, advanced from the master bedroom to the kitchen, and withdrew a cold bottle of water from the refrigerator's interior door. He needed to stay hydrated in case he and Sandy enjoyed a long afternoon in her bed. He almost unscrewed the bottle top, but remembered patience. He would sip at it as he maneuvered the Jag up 75. By the time he approached the Tennessee border, he'd be ready for a drive-thru lunch and a Diet Coke. Or a Diet Mountain Dew if he decided to hit the Taco Bell he found the last time he'd driven up to see where Sandy and Don lived.

He placed the stick-pad note for Elizabeth on the mantle in the living room, but remembered that at five-four his wife could easily miss it. He couldn't have that. So he picked up the note and took it back to the kitchen. If he stuck it on the refrigerator door up high enough and folded the bottom half up so the kids couldn't read it, Elizabeth couldn't miss it, and the kids didn't need to know.

As he locked the front door and walked out the brick walkway and across the driveway pavers to the metallic-blue Jaguar sedan that would again take him to Chattanooga, Crafton wondered how she was waiting for him. Was she in the shower, lathering herself in scented body gel, counting the minutes to his 'surprise' arrival on his long-awaited fortieth birthday? Or was she pulling together the ingredients for a 'surprise' brunch on the veranda which opened off those two sets of sliding doors overlooking Lookout Mountain? Or was she still asleep, having finally drifted off at four a.m. after hours of eager reminiscence of the months together before Don McKay—

He needed to concentrate. He opened the driver door, descended into the tan leather driver's seat, carefully placed the duffel bag in the passenger seat, put the water bottle in the cupholder, and gently pulled the door shut. Elizabeth and the kids could wake up at any minute. No need to help with that now. He started the engine and seconds later he was on his way down the curved drive to Felton Parkway, entering the street while plugging Sandy's address into the GPS. Not that he needed the directions, but it was always nice to have an ETA.

Elizabeth and the kids would miss him, of course. He had even brushed little Billy's teeth last night, giving his son one last close moment with his dad. Billy would cherish it one day. There was comfort in that knowledge. A minute later the Jaguar passed the BP at the right corner before the entrance ramp to 75 North. On the ramp he pressed the gas.

He hadn't brushed Emily's teeth because she was six now and very independent. Crafton was sad about that. But at the same time, it was good to know she didn't need her dad. He reached eighty on the speedometer before finishing his merge. He set the cruise control for eighty-one and reached for the water bottle, using his left thigh to control the wheel while twisting the too-full container carefully, gently, with both hands to avoid spilling water on his lap. It might not dry before his arrival at Sandy's, and that would absolutely not do.

Twenty minutes later, as he passed Lake Allatoona, he barely remembered to take the north exit for a quick stop at the lake. At the end of the exit ramp he turned left and drove the three hundred yards to the parking lot for the public boat ramp. There was only one other vehicle, a red Dodge Ram pickup. It was empty. Someone was out enjoying their boat.

Crafton stepped out of the Jaguar, cell phone in hand, and walked toward the dock that ran parallel to the boat ramp. As he strolled, he turned off his phone. He stepped onto the dock, advanced to its end, and lobbed the phone underhanded like a softball, as far out over the water as he could. It landed flat with a smack, and then disappeared into the murky depths of the clay-misted water.

Returning to the Jag, Crafton knew he would miss being able to look at Sandy's pictures. Billy's and Emily's too. But that was what new phones were for. Goodbye, T-Mobile. Hello, Verizon. Goodbye, Facebook. After all, he would have Sandy's password anyway, and wouldn't need to look at her pictures anymore. No need for a billboard saying 'Crafton Kelly Is Here.' He wasn't there. He was forty now. He had a promise to keep. And new pictures to take.

SHOEBOX LOVE

He saw the old Florsheim shoebox in the back of the attic, resting beneath the lamp with the male cardinal standing sentinel under the ancient incandescent bulb. He left it there. He hadn't been looking for it.

He'd been looking for the white plastic stepstool. In the morning he'd replace the dim bulb above the master vanity on Amanda's side. Best to use the morning energy and three eggs over medium to pursue the bulb change before watering the flowers.

At three in the morning he awoke. He'd had a dream. In the dream there were four torn scraps of paper, a word written in black cursive on each, staring at him from the coffee table he hadn't kept after college. He didn't know where that coffee table went in 1971. But he knew where the scraps of paper went. They'd lived with him in secret for forty-nine years, hidden in four attics across the decades of children, grandchildren, and the kind of love that doesn't live in a shoebox.

Careful not to awaken Amanda, he lowered himself out of bed and into his waiting slippers. He padded through the open doorway and down the hall to the ceiling's attic door that waited, like his slippers, to return him to the endless road of regret.

He grabbed the pull cord and lowered the door until he could grip both sides of the ladder, extending it noiselessly to the floor. The WD-40 had yet to fail him. He'd happily do a commercial for the WD-40 people. Such was his gratitude on many three-in-the-morning journeys to 1971 and the kind of love that does indeed live in shoeboxes.

At the top of the attic steps he rested to let his heart slow its staccato, then reached for the flashlight atop the trunk that had carried all three kids' clothes to all three kids' colleges.

He shuffled to the attic's rear, careful to avoid Billy's old Big Wheel. He lifted the cardinal lamp and set it gently on the floor to the left of the Florsheim box. As he reached for the box, the old panic set in, the panic he'd felt in 1971, in the days and weeks that stretched into months and years, the panic whispering "How are you going to live this life without *her*?"

The panic had been tardy in 1971. Three days late, to be exact.

He opened the box and retrieved the four scraps of yellow lined paper. Sitting cross-legged despite the pain in his hips, he spread the pieces in a row on the wood-plank floor. One at a time, he shone the light on each scrap. The first, the only one with a capital letter, said 'Do', the loop of the D caressing the 'o', carrying them both toward the second word, which featured a single letter, graceful and deserving: 'I'. The third bore the awful verb: 'bore'. The last revealed the end: 'you?'

He lifted the flashlight. "Do I bore you?" he whispered.

He'd found the note under his dormitory door after attending a mixer as rush co-chairman of his fraternity. He'd shaken his head in youthful wonder. How on God's earth could she think she *bored* him? She didn't. Naturally.

Three nights later she broke up with him before dessert. Devastated, he'd pleaded and then surrendered, returning to his room in a fit of hurt, tearing the note into four small pieces.

Later, when her best friend told him about the rumor that he'd cheated on her, his righteous fury was that of a young man victimized. It wasn't his fault that there were devious and jealous people in the world.

Now, sitting on the attic floor with a note in four pieces, he remembered that it hadn't been his fault that she was told the lie about him. He wouldn't have cheated on her with a gun to his head.

What *was* his fault was that she believed it. She was hurt. She'd asked the right question.

Do I bore you?

There were two answers: the one that puts love in a shoebox, or the one that lives in the sun and rain like forever flowers.

He closed his eyes and thanked her again—wherever she and her own forever flowers might be—for teaching him to make the question unnecessary for the love of his life, who slept alone downstairs during his annual date with fortunate regret.

QUARTERBACK

"Y ou probably don't know this about me, but when I was in sixth grade I was the backup quarterback of the middle school football team at Chapel Hill Country Day.

"Yes. That's right, Katie. I *know* I played soccer in high school. If you'll just listen, I'll tell you *why* I played soccer after sixth grade. I—

"No, *not* why I played football. I played football because I was expected by your grandfather and especially your great-grandfather to play football. So I played football in sixth grade, and now I've answered your question anyway. But I'm going to tell you why I played *soccer* in high school.

"Well, Katie, it's because right now I think you need to hear it. Bob can put the kids to bed just this once, right? So you can spend a few minutes on the phone with your dad?

"I meant no disrespect to Bob. Just give me five or ten minutes here, okay? Okay. So I was the backup quarterback, and the starting quarterback was a big eighth-grader named Tommy Jensen. Tommy was over six feet tall, already pushing six-three in fact. He had a cannon for an arm, as I totally planned to have by the time I too was six-three and firing touchdown passes and getting the girls. I don't know if Dad expected me to get the girls, but Granddad did because he played quarterback in college and was a lot happier to talk about the old days of football and girls than he was to talk about the old days in the war. So he talked about the girls, and about the importance of becoming a quarterback if I wanted to be a leader in life. My dad wasn't a quarterback, but he was a star tight end and linebacker. Sort of the same difference. Seeing as how he was my dad, he didn't talk so much about the girls. Not with your grandmother around.

"Yes, Katie, this is going somewhere. Please. So about six weeks into the season, I still hadn't played a down at quarterback in a game. It didn't matter if we were winning thirty-five to nothing; Tommy Jensen was playing quarterback. It was a good thing I hadn't played in a game, actually, because I only knew one play: 48 Off Tackle. You see, I didn't like the idea of playing quarterback in a game, because I didn't like playing quarterback in practice or anywhere at all. I didn't know the plays, even though I was supposed to know them by studying at home. I couldn't throw the ball very far, not yet, even though a quarterback is supposed to be able to throw the ball or else the defense will recognize such a colossal weakness and put all eleven guys on the line of scrimmage, making you punt twelve times in one game.

"So our sixth game arrived and it was a road game. The opponent was Belcher Middle School... yes... yes, Belcher. It's a small town in North Carolina near Raleigh. So we arrived there on the bus, dressed to play as always since our return trips were short enough not to shower and change after a game. But as we approached the field that night, we were directed to an area near one of the end zones where there were two men waiting next to what looked like the kind of scales they use to weigh you at the doctor's office. Immediately I developed a pit in my stomach. I'd heard that some county youth organizations required a weigh-in because there was a weight limit for middle-school football in those counties. Sure enough, there was a hand-painted sign next to the scale that said the weight limit for middle school football was 150 pounds. No, I thought. Please,

God, *no*. I looked with deep dread at Tommy Jensen, who was third in line to be weighed, about ten guys ahead of me. There was no way Tommy weighed less than one-seventy-five or one-eighty. I prayed. More than any time in any church pew to that point in my life, I prayed. If Tommy Jensen was disqualified for being too big, I would have to be the starting quarterback. Coach Wallace would turn to me in his Army crew cut, pull me to the side by my wrist like he always did to older guys when he was pissed at them, and say 'You're starting, Stephen. Are you ready? Get warmed up.'

"Five minutes later, Tommy Jensen was disqualified for being over the weight limit. My first reaction, aside from the fear of anticipation, was that I was mad at Tommy for being so big. And then Coach Wallace said the words that terrified me so, as if he clearly expected me to be Tommy Jensen. You have to remember, Katie, that the difference between an eighth-grade boy and a sixth-grade boy can be like the difference between Mount Everest and a hill by an apple orchard. At least it's like that in football and basketball. I couldn't have been Tommy Jensen that night even if I *was* prepared. And I was more unprepared for that moment than for any other moment of my life.

"There's only one guy on a football team who's supposed to know *every* play in the playbook, plus what every player *does* on every play in the playbook. Actually, that's not true. *Two* guys are supposed to know every play in the playbook. The starting quarterback and the backup quarterback. There's a reason why it's called 'backup'. Sort of like the co-pilot of an airplane, the backup quarterback is supposed to be able to steer the plane if something happens to the pilot. Maybe not throw as many passes as the quarterback, but be able to run every play in the playbook to give the team a chance to win without, you know, the starting quarterback.

"Yes, Katie, there's a point to the story. Patience. Your husband is a talented father. So my heart was beating a mile a minute. I asked Eddie Farber, the team's best receiver, to play catch with me so I could warm up. He laughed. He was, after all, an eighth-grader and a starter who caught three touchdown passes the previous week at home against Orange Prep.

"Yes, Katie, I remember details like that. I'm describing a traumatic memory for you, as your father. Details help.

"Okay, fine, so you don't need to know who we played the previous week. But it matters that Eddie Farber caught three touchdown passes the previous week, and as an eighth-grader wasn't going to be caught dead warming up the little sixth-grader replacing Tommy Jensen for a whole four quarters of endless torture. Remember I only knew one play.

"Yes. 48 Off Tackle. You *are* listening. That's my girl. So I got Jonathan Wheeler, my classmate and the third-string center, to play catch with me. My hands were shaking so badly that I almost dropped the ball every time I threw Jonathan one of my wounded ducks.

"Wounded duck. It's a wobbly pass from a quarterback who can't throw spirals. My hands weren't big enough to throw a spiral. You have to have your forefinger pointed toward the north end of the football to—

"Got it. Detail. Okay. So the game started. We lost the coin toss and kicked off. Belcher scored a touchdown in six or seven plays, their quarterback expertly executing every run and every passing play, completing the drive on a keeper around right end for the touchdown. It wouldn't be long now. You can't slow down time. When the kick return team took the field, I prayed for us to fumble. Anything to keep me from being in that huddle with ten eighth-graders looking at me like the imposter I knew I was.

"No, Katie, I wasn't literally an imposter. I was the backup quarterback and everybody knew that. But I'd never practiced a single down with the starters. And even though I had practiced more than 48 Off Tackle, it was the only play I knew by heart. I was supposed to know about twenty-five plays. Tommy Jensen knew twenty-five plays. So anyway, our returner got creamed at about the twenty-yard line on the return, but he held onto the ball, dammit. Coach Wallace pulled me up to the sideline—well, 'dragged' might be more accurate—and reminded me to fasten my chin strap. Then he said he would send in the plays with runners. I was relieved when he said, 'I'll give you the first one now. 48 Off Tackle, Left.'

"Well, I have to tell you, Katie. I was relieved. So I ran out onto the field, confident that the first play would go well. I got into the huddle. I looked around at the older faces. Then I called my first play as a quarterback in an official game. 'Forty-eight off tackle left,' I said with authority. Eddie Farber laughed. 'Snap your chin strap on, dip.'

"Well, Katie, that sort of ruined the moment for me. Being called a dip was about the worst thing you could be called in middle school, except for 'faggot' of course. The whole bunch of guys laughed, though a couple of them were probably just being good-natured. I felt myself blush kind of hot, remembering that Coach Wallace told me to fasten my chin strap right before the good news that 48 Off Tackle would be the first play from scrimmage. I needed to regain my authority, so I repeated the play. 'Forty eight off tackle left,' I said in as low a voice as I could muster as I fumbled to snap my chin strap. 'Ready… Break!'

"Nobody moved. A couple of guys snickered. Then Eddie Farber did it again. 'We're not deaf, dip. What's the count?'

"This time nobody laughed. Now they had serious doubts. About me. And we hadn't even run a play yet. I wished I was in eighth grade so I could tell Eddie Farber where to stick it. But that's not how middle school hierarchy works. 'On three,' I said. 'Ready... Break!' I clapped my hands once like we were all supposed to do in unison to break the huddle and advance to the line of scrimmage. Except nobody else clapped their hands, in unison or any way at all.

"God, Katie. No, I'm not asking for a pity party. Not forty-five years later. I'm telling you this story because of *your* situation, not mine. Okay?

"Thank you. So... with total dread I approached the line of scrimmage. The first thing I noticed was how big the entire Belcher defense looked. And their middle linebacker was licking his chops, growling and jumping around with his fists in front of him. He wanted me to think he was going to blitz and drive my face into the dirt. The second thing I noticed was that Eldred Schmidt's behind was a lot bigger than Jonathan Wheeler's. I was going to get lost under center. I had no idea where to put my hands. So I just put them under his butt and prayed he wouldn't miss. I started the count. The snap would happen on the third 'Hut!', but there was something about the meaningless word 'Blue' that always made me want to yell it in practice. And a number after 'Blue' sounded nice, like when the microphones in a Steelers game would pick up Terry Bradshaw's voice calling the signals. So I began:

"'Blue, forty-six!' I yelled from under center. Eldred Schmidt's helmet turned to the right, like he was wondering what the heck 'Blue, forty-six' meant. But it sounded good. I repeated it. 'Blue, forty-six!'. Then I yelled 'Set!', except I drew out the 'e' part for about two seconds. Then came the big ones: 'Hut! Hut!... Hut!' Just as I uttered the third 'Hut' to start the play, the middle linebacker stepped into the gap between Eldred Schmidt and Eric Jackson at left guard. Eldred snapped the ball. I guessed my hands were smaller than Tommy Jensen's, or else my arms were shorter, but the football glanced off my left pinky and fell horrifyingly to the ground. I panicked and tried to pick it up, but I was pulverized by the middle line-backer before I could touch it. He pile-drived me backwards about two yards, and then pancaked me onto the ground. The wind was knocked all the way out of me by the impact. As I gasped for air, I heard the Belcher side of the field erupt in loud cheering that kept going long enough, punctuated by a second burst of cheers, for me to know that somebody for Belcher had picked up the ball and either pranced—if he was a linebacker or safety—or lumbered—if he was a lineman—into the end zone for a two-touchdown lead less than two minutes into the game. The middle linebacker climbed off me, but not before adding to my indignity, whispering 'You're gonna have a long night, pussy.' He didn't yell it, because a referee was prob-ably nearby, but he said it so matter-of-factly that I believed him. No, check that. I didn't believe him. I knew he was right. There's a difference.

"What do you mean, the kids can't brush their teeth without you? How old's Colleen now? Eight? All right. No, I don't want to say good night now. I'll wait.

***

"Yes, I'm still here. Got caught up on some Tolstoy while you were gone.

"Sorry. I know you're in no mood for sarcasm. My bad, Ka-tie. I won't take much longer, I promise. So when I got back to the sideline, Eldred Schmidt was waiting for me. The older guys all called him Schmidty, but there was an unwritten rule that sixth graders didn't get to do that. 'How did you miss my *snap*?' he asked, in a tone that was like saying 'I can't believe you totaled my *car*.' I said maybe we could practice a few times during the kickoff, but he was gone already. He wasn't really asking a question.

"I risked a glance at your granddad and grandma. They were in the second row of the bleachers behind our bench. Grandma looked at me the way she always did, and that helped for the three seconds before I made eye contact with my dad. You see, your granddad had a way of letting me know he loved me in spite of my failures. Later, in high school, if I scored two goals in a soccer game, he'd tell me he was proud of me and knew I would find more time to practice heading the ball, because if I'd practiced heading the ball more, I would've scored a hat trick on that beautiful corner kick by Jon Massey. Then he would say 'Next time.' In a millisecond I would go from the euphoria of scoring two goals in a three-to-two victory to the shame of not heading in my third goal on that beautiful corner kick by Jon Massey. So you can imagine how your granddad was look-ing at me after fumbling the snap on my first play as a starting quarterback. In that look I didn't see any difference between my dad and Eddie Farber.

"No, I didn't read anything into anything, Katie. You can drop that right now. I've never told this story to anybody but your mom. I need this at fifty-seven just as much as you do at thirty-two.

"Yes. You do. So indulge your father for a few more min-utes. Roll your eyes like you're sixteen, whatever you want. But listen. So on the second kickoff, our return guy, I forget who it was—maybe Ricky Lambert—made it out to about the forty. This time I had my chin strap fastened, because somehow it didn't bust when Dick Butkus almost killed me. Coach Wallace stopped me when I was about to run onto the field. He put his arm around me, making me feel even smaller than I was, and said 'Don't worry about it. Just focus on securing the football.' As if I wasn't already focused like a laser on securing the foot-ball. That didn't help. Then he said, 'Run 34 Counter.' Uh-oh, I thought. Of course I didn't know how to run 34 Counter. I didn't even know what it looked like, even though I'd probably seen our tailback Jamie Kolb score on that play a couple of times. I knew it was a running play. So was 48 Off Tackle. So... I decided to run 48 Off Tackle. After all, we hadn't really run 48 Off Tackle yet. You know, because I fumbled the snap. Reasonable, right? If Coach Wallace got pissed, I could tell him I audibled. Not that I had any idea how quarterbacks audible at the line of scrimmage. I just knew the color commentators talked about audibles, and that it had to do with reading the defense and changing plays to cross up the opposition.

"So in the huddle I said 'Forty-eight Off Tackle, Left.' Nobody objected because we never really ran it the first time. Then I remembered the count. 'On two,' I said, trying to sound like I knew what I was doing. I said 'Ready... Break!' This time the other guys said 'Break', but not with the metaphorical exclamation point if you know what I mean. Pretty half-hearted, but better than me alone. This time I got to the line of scrimmage and the middle linebacker was dancing back and forth to both sides of Eldred Schmidt. I decided to wait until he danced to my right before yelling two quick huts, so I could secure the snap and move quickly to my left to hand the ball off to Jamie Kolb. There was normalcy in Jamie Kolb. I needed normalcy and I needed it quick.

"After I yelled out 'Blue, fifty-two'—fifty-two was for the heck of it again, so I could sound like I knew what I was doing—the middle linebacker danced to my left but then quickly to my right. I took advantage and yelled out two quick huts. Eldred snapped the ball, but softly this time like he was looking for my hands. I secured the ball and rushed to my left, sticking it into Jamie Kolb's belly just as he arrived behind left tackle. Jamie did the rest, and gained four yards before sure enough, the middle linebacker brought him down with an ankle assist from Belcher's really fat right defensive tackle. Four yards! Katie, I was in heaven. The game, win or lose, wasn't going to depend on me. As long as I could run 48 Off Tackle, the game wouldn't depend on me. That was the key thing, the way to work my way through a nightmare.

"Back in the huddle, it was second down and six. Then the runner arrived. The runner was a player subbing in so he could give me the play from Coach Wall—

"Well, excuse me, Katie. I can't assume you know all the terminology of a football game. You never wanted to watch with me on Sunday afternoons.

"Okay. Touche. Those were your ice-skating competitions. I still have all the pictures your mom took.

"No, not in the storage unit. They're in a scrapbook your mom made. I keep it in my desk. I was always so proud of you.

"That's a cheap shot, Katie. I was proud of the Steelers in a different way. Please. Let me continue. So the runner said '34 Counter, Right.' This time all the guys in the huddle knew the play call. But I didn't know the play. It probably involved a handoff to Jamie Kolb, yes, and that was good. But where? What angle? Behind what block? Would I wheel and retreat to the runner, or go diagonally? Do I fake a handoff to the fullback first? I had no idea. And a sixth-grader trying to pretend he knew what he was doing couldn't ask ten eighth-graders how to run the play. Well, the runner was Todd Melkovich, and he was in seventh grade, but you know what I mean. Low end of the totem pole and all that.

"So I called 48 Off Tackle, Right. Eddie Farber was first to object. '34 Counter Right, dip,' he said. I decided I'd better be honest. I only practiced with these guys on tackling drills, so they didn't know I didn't know all the plays.

"'I only know 48 Off Tackle. Just two plays,' I said. 'That's one play, dip,' Eddie said. But then Jamie Kolb helped me out. 'Eddie, it's two. Left and Right. Two plays. Cut the dip some slack.'

"Now Katie, ordinarily if someone called a guy a dip in front of other guys, the dip wouldn't be grateful. But I was grateful to Jamie Kolb right then. Maybe he helped me because I only knew the play that could give him a hundred-yard game if we ran it thirty times. I don't know. But I needed an eighth-grader to have my back, and so it didn't matter that he called me a dip. He called me a dip while defending me. So… bolstered by an eighth-grader's support, I repeated the call. 48 Off Tackle, Right. I said it with authority. With equal authority I said the count was on one. And then I learned that the eighth-graders respected Jamie Kolb. When I said 'Ready… Break!' there was both unison and enthusiasm. I approached the line and this time I didn't care where the middle linebacker was. I called out 'Blue, twenty-five' twice, once to my left and once to my right, then a quick 'Hut!' as Eldred Schmidt snapped the ball right into my waiting hands. I wheeled and delivered the ball with emphasis to Jamie Kolb, who exploded through the line for nine yards and a first down. As we returned to the huddle, Jamie looked at me with a smile, as if to say 'Hook me up, and I'll hook you up, dip.' It was exhilarating. We were marching now.

"And then Coach Wallace called a timeout. He came running onto the field—he was in shape in a crew-cut Army sergeant kind of way—and boy was he pissed. I mean steam-coming-out-of-his-ears blowing his stack pissed. He grabbed me by the facemask and jerked my helmet to within two inches of his red face. There was spittle gathering in both corners of his mouth. Then—

"Yes. I know he was very calm in his history classes. The football field isn't a history classroom, Katie. There's a certain… intensity, like in basketball. And the Marines. So anyway, Coach Wallace went ballistic. He told me if I wanted to be the head coach of this football team, I should just say so. Naturally I didn't say so. He said when he calls 34 Counter, he means 34

Counter and I'm off the team if I do this again. He still had me by the facemask. I snuck a glance past him toward your grand-dad and grandma. My mom's hands were covering her cheeks. No surprise there. My dad's arms were folded, the expression on his face saying I was getting what I deserved and would learn from it.

"But then something surprising happened. Eddie Farber raised his hand and said 'Coach, can I say something?' Coach Wallace released my facemask and turned to face Eddie. He said nothing. He just folded his arms like my dad, as if to say 'This better be good.' Eddie then proceeded to blow my cover. 'Coach, Stephen doesn't know the plays. He only knows 48 Off Tackle. Both directions though,' he said, as if to mitigate the in-formation in my favor. I appreciated that. It was as if he didn't think I was a dip.

"Coach Wallace turned back to me and asked if it was true that I only knew 48 Off Tackle. I confessed on the spot. I was kind of relieved. It's a terrible thing for a backup quarterback to hold in. Especially in front of a bunch of eighth-graders. I braced myself for the fury that was about to arrive like a hur-ricane on the coastline of my face. The spittle might even fly.

"But then he surprised all of us. He unfolded his arms and said, 'Well, we do run that play fifteen or twenty times a game.' We all looked at each other in amazement. He continued. 'You know, someone once said that if you're really good at some-thing, it doesn't matter if your opponent knows what you're going to do. You'll succeed because you're so damned good at it. Who here thinks we can run 48 Off Tackle all night, left, right, left, right. Just run it down their throats.'

"I already knew that's what we were going to do, because it's all I knew how to do. I looked over at the bench and saw Tommy Jensen sitting there with his head down. He had his own problems tonight, and none of them were his fault. He loved football a whole lot more than I did, and this night was already killing him. I needed to stop being jealous of him, because right now he was jealous of *me*. Little old sixth-grader *me*. I raised my hand. So did everybody else, Jamie Kolb the highest. We could run 48 Off Tackle all night because every one of us would do our jobs. We could do that for each other. And I could do that for Tommy Jensen, who could never have this game back, just like one day he could never have eighth grade back, and one day not long after that he could never have being a quarterback back.

"So we voted to run 48 Off Tackle every play. Every single down. Coach Wallace ran back to the sideline. I looked back at your granddad and surprised him with a smile.

"We ran the next 48 Off Tackle to the left, and Jamie rumbled for fifteen yards because Eldred Schmidt cut the middle linebacker off at the knees when Jamie cut back against the grain. Three plays later we scored when Jamie burst into the backfield and Eddie Farber, who wasn't usually interested in blocking from the wide receiver position, attacked the Belcher safety like a man obsessed, driving him into the ground as Jamie sprinted past the goal line. We went for two because we didn't have a kicker. 48 Off Tackle, Left. Jamie went in standing up. The Belcher middle linebacker had to leave the game. Want to know why? Because after I handed the ball off to Jamie, I went straight at the dip and hit him with everything I had, which was all that a hundred-and-twenty-five pounds can deliver. What I had was enough to put him on the ground. It was exhilarating, Katie. Especially for a kid who didn't like playing football.

"We lost the game, thirty-six to thirty-two. But we scored four touchdowns and converted every single two-point conversion. I didn't fumble any more snaps, and I never threw a pass. What was that Clint Eastwood movie where Eastwood says 'A good man always knows his limitations'? I can't think of it right off the top—

"Right! Magnum Force. He says it twice to Hal Holbrook, the superior officer who's taking the law into his own hands. And he was right. I knew my limitations. I threw wounded ducks, not spirals. And I only knew one play. But I could run that one play left or right with the best of them. The linemen could block it left or right. Jamie Kolb could run it left or right, or through and past. Eddie Farber could be a blocker. Eldred Schmidt could move his big feet fast enough to cut Butkus's legs out from under him. And Coach Wallace could make the best of a bad situation. This was more than any of us knew when the night started.

"Thanks, Katie. But you know the best part of it for me? After the game, Tommy Jensen sat down next to me on the bus. Yep. This big eighth-grader, who had to miss one of a very finite set of games in eighth grade because some self-important grownups didn't have enough to do, sat next to me and gave me a quiet high five. He was a quiet guy, Tommy Jensen was, and we both knew that if he hadn't been disqualified just for being a big kid, we would've won the game. Then he asked me a question I've never forgotten. It's a question I always wanted my dad to ask, but he didn't. 'Do you like playing football, Stephen?'

"I could tell he already knew the answer. 'No,' I said. 'But I love the Steelers.'

"'What do you like to play, man?' He called me 'man'. Not 'dip'. Katie, you have no idea what that means to a sixth-grade boy sitting next to the starting quarterback.

"'Soccer,' I said. 'I like to go down to Forest Hills Park and play soccer.'

"Tommy looked at me for a few seconds. 'Then why don't you play soccer, man? Not right now, because you back me up and I'm glad about that. But next year. I'll be at the high school and I'll have a new backup, or maybe the backup will be me. You go play soccer, man. Because you love it.'

"Katie, I honestly had never even thought of playing soccer anywhere but at Forest Hills Park or in gym class. I was too afraid of your granddad to tell him I liked being a Steelers fan but didn't want to be a Steeler. But Tommy Jensen called me 'man'. And if Tommy Jensen called me 'man', then I was going to be one.

"After the season I told your granddad I was going to play soccer the next year in seventh grade. I made sure your grandma was there, of course. I'm not stupid. And guess what? He surprised me, like Coach Wallace did. He said, 'Why did you play football if you don't like it? Is that why you didn't study the plays? You didn't like playing the game?' I said 'Yes, sir.' He said 'And you played a position like quarterback anyway, with all that responsibility? And everyone counting on you?' 'Yes, sir,' I said.

"And then he said one thing before lifting the Durham Sun newspaper back in front of his face that late afternoon. 'Tough guy, you are, Stephen. You're going to go places, son.'

"I floated up the stairs to my room, knowing my career as a quarterback had ended with an honorable discharge. You've seen the soccer pictures in my office downtown. I loved soccer, and soccer loved me. If it hadn't been for some officious jerks in Belcher, North Carolina wrecking one night of Tommy Jensen's life, I might've dutifully ridden the bench for another six years on the gridiron to please my father, not knowing how much he loved me. Not knowing he was proud of me. And last week I was friended on Facebook by Tommy Jensen. We're going to dinner when he's in town next month on business. He's senior vice president of a company that sells football equipment to high schools. He loves it. Ten minutes after I accepted

Tommy's friend request, I got one from Eldred Schmidt. One of those 'mutual friends' things, I guess. You know, the center. When I wrote him back on Messenger, he asked me to call him Schmidty. I felt like I was eleven again, in all the best ways.

"No. I haven't told anyone this story since your mom died. I know you're upset right now, and you have every right to be. But tell me the truth. If you'd made partner, would you have been happier?

"You're answering a question with a question, Katie. The answer is no. I wouldn't have been happier if I'd been a starting quarterback, team captain, and had the head cheerleader fall in love with me. *You* imagine that, not me. It would've meant six more years playing a sport I didn't like playing, in this one life I had the chance to live. It would've meant actively avoiding something I loved. And I was a soccer player in college when I met your mother. Think of that. You wouldn't exist without this story being true. I've had the life I wanted because of one night when I was eleven years old. That's not something most people can say when they're pushing sixty. I asked you a question, because I've told you a story tonight that you should've heard when you were majoring in Art History. That's my fault. I owed you this story then, because the Katie you were then would've listened. You *hate* being a lawyer, Katie. Even your mother knew that. So today's news at the firm isn't a setback. It's an opportunity. Why can't you *see* that?

"Well then. I'm sorry you feel that way. You used to like my dumb stories. I'm just sorry I never told you this one when you were twenty. When you were twenty you wanted to run an art gallery in New York or Paris or maybe San Francisco. You said it all the time. And you thought I was the wisest man in the world. Yes, I should've told you this dumb story then. Funny. Most people think their parents develop wisdom later in life. Somehow I've lost mine, haven't I?

"I think I've let you down, Katie. Some day I'll figure out when I finished doing that. Have a good night, honey. Schmidty asked me to give him a call. There's always room in my life for new friendships—including the ones that are overdue—and sometimes, at least sometimes, there's nothing better than reliving our dumbest stories."

A TASTE OF
SPAGHETTI

✳ ✳ ✳

T he sky went dark as the credits rolled northward on the blackening screen. Miller could go now.

He rose from the charcoal-gray sofa, picked up the remote from the coffee table, and stared down at what was left of the spaghetti. She had made it exactly a year ago, before leaving for the night shift at the hospital. He still had the yellow post-it. It said "I can't wait to get home in the morning. Love ya!" He had put the spaghetti into the freezer after reading the note and placing it square in the middle of the aluminum foil. He would read it 365 times in the next year. Then he would decide whether she and Bob Sackin would live or die.

He let the credits continue to roll because he liked Ennio Morricone. The haunting beauty of the music helped him with his resolve. He returned the remote to the coffee table, silently, as if Laura and Bob would hear him from Bob's house in Port Royal, and picked up the spaghetti plate. Carrying it to the kitchen and setting it in the sink without the fork moving a millimeter, he made his decision. 365 days had passed by even faster than the 241 days Laura had shared Miller's house with him, and of course far more swiftly than the six days in which he knew about Bob after coming home three days early from his trip to Chicago and finding Laura's note on Bob's spaghetti.

He had flown back to Chicago that night, panicked at the new fact, new to him anyway, that his life would not be spent with her, that his children would not also be hers, that she would not be holding his hand as he took his last breath in the comfort of knowing they would be together as souls forever upon the last breath of her own.

They had known he knew as soon as she asked Bob if he liked the spaghetti. What they had not known was that they had a year to persuade Miller to spare their lives. When she had called him the next morning after not being able to wait to get home to Bob, he answered the bleating of his cell phone with an instruction: "Leave the spaghetti. At least leave the spaghetti. I want to try your spaghetti." She had protested that he was being dramatic in his sarcasm, or maybe it was sarcastic in his drama. He couldn't remember which. And she had been sorry, so sorry. It was just a fling, she said.

Miller rinsed the spaghetti plate, 365 days after freezing it. He scrubbed it clean with a drop of Palmolive and an old Brillo pad. Holding the plate to the light to make sure there was no food on it, satisfied that it was clean, he smashed it on the stainless steel rim of the sink, shards clattering and clinking onto the Spanish tile floor before settling back into the atmosphere of Ennio Morricone.

"It was just a fling," he whispered.

He turned and opened the drawer to the right of the refrigerator. He reached to the back of the drawer and retrieved the black Walther his father had given him on his twenty-fifth birthday, three weeks after Miller was robbed at gunpoint in a home invasion back when he lived in the beaten-up cottage in Burton.

They would be surprised, of course. Shocked, even. Miller knew that he didn't seem like the type to take drastic action on anything at all. Yet in fifteen minutes they would see what he had in him. And so would he in less than one.

He picked up his cell phone and dialed her number. She answered by saying his name. She sounded friendly. Miller chose the same tone.

"I just finished the spaghetti," he said. "Thank you."

"David, no!" She sounded frantic.

"It was delicious," Miller said.

"David, just hold on. Stay right there. Don't you *do* anything! I will be right—"

Miller was surprised, just for a millisecond, to recognize the love in her voice. And then he was gone, beating the last descending strings of another Morricone masterpiece.

PROUD BOY

* * *

Harley Francis's cell phone bleated at 1:47 in the morning. "Here we go," he whispered. "Trouble."

He sent the call to voicemail and heaved himself out of bed. Rhonda didn't stir. She'd come in from Jackson's room just twenty minutes ago. Five hours she spent in the boy's room! Not that it mattered where she slept. They hadn't laid a hand on each other since three weeks earlier, before she said she was voting for Biden.

He'd gone to sleep with his jeans and socks on. This time wasn't because of a bender. It was time-saving preparation for the call to arms, so all he needed to do was strap his Kevlar vest over his white tee shirt, lace up his boots, throw on the camouflage jacket, and head out the door.

The guns were loaded and ready, the assault sitting tall at attention in the Ram's front passenger seat while the .38 leaned sideways facing the right dash with its butt in the passenger cupholder. He didn't bother with the seatbelt. The courthouse was only a mile away; there would be no traffic aside from his brothers in arms. And the cops, of course. The anarchists would be there on foot and acting crazy, so for sure the men in blue would be happy to see a big Ram pickup arriving.

When he saw the crowd up ahead in front of the courthouse, he was disappointed to see no commotion. Was he the first freedom fighter to arrive? If so, he decided, it was to his advantage. He parked on the Main Street curb in front of the Chamber of Commerce building, about half a football field from the action, which featured a hundred or so candles and some faggy waving and singing. Fine.

He grabbed the weapons and jumped out of the white pickup, stuffing the handgun into his left pocket and throwing the strap of the AR-15 over his right shoulder. Stepping to the rear of the truck, he picked up the two-gallon container of gasoline. The matches were already in his left fatigue pocket, another testament to Harley's capacity for preparation.

Instead of approaching the protest directly, he hurried straight behind the Chamber of Commerce building and onto the darkened service road that ran parallel to Main. This way he would stroll unobserved to the back of the courthouse, douse the entire length of the two-hundred-year-old building, set it ablaze, then drop the three Black Lives Matter fliers randomly, not too close together, each with just enough gasoline droplets saturating them to match what was used to start the fire. The conclusion by experienced arson investigators would be simple: the anarchists carried the open container of gas while also toting a supply of the fliers they'd been putting under windshield wipers all week. Careless, sloppy, and evidence that the country needed a greater commitment to law and order.

Minutes later, he finished the generous dousing of the historic building, a wood structure built on a thick foundation of crushed seashells and plaster. He stepped backward about twenty feet so he could see the full breadth of the building. If he lit the matches going left to right, he could ignite the left corner, which he imagined to be an end zone, then the thirty yard line, midfield, the other thirty yard line, and the right corner (the other end zone), then walk around the right side of the building and join the fracas which his brothers would be initiating at any minute. Once the blaze started, they could open fire on the anarchists who'd set it.

He started walking toward the left end zone, withdrawing a book of long wooden matches from his right pocket. He was almost there when a little voice stopped him.

"Sir?"

It sounded like a child. He turned, knowing that after two in the morning it couldn't be a kid. It just couldn't.

Before him stood a little blond-haired girl of about six. It was dark, so he couldn't see whether the object she hugged in her arms was a teddy bear or some kind of blanket or 'woobie'. Her feet were bare, as if she'd just gotten out of bed and went out the door. Nothing about her seemed lost or hungry. She was just outside.

"What are you doing out here, sweetheart?" Harley asked, concerned. He looked down at the gas can, and set it down behind him. "Do your parents know you're outside? They must be worried. It's—it's the middle of the night."

"Elroy heard something and told me to look out the window. What are you doing, sir?"

Her voice annoyed him. Something about it suggested that she knew exactly what he was doing. It was the way she said 'doing', as if her voice climbed a hill to utter the two syllables, then descended the hill to say 'sir'.

"Is Elroy your bear, sweetie?"

"He's not a bear. He's a turtle."

"I—I see. Well, I think you and Elroy need to go back home. Do you live in that—"

"What are you doing, sir?"

The hill again. '—*DOING*, sir?'

He was losing valuable time. Critical time. But he couldn't light the match in front of the girl. It was a quandary. Harley didn't like quandaries.

"Honey, I'm doing important work. For our country. And you need to go back to bed."

Harley made out a smile on the girl's face. Something about it made him feel sick. It was a smile that didn't belong on a child's face.

"Y—you need to go back to bed, little girl. You and El—"

"Can I start it?"

The hill again. This time the rise was on 'start'. Harley felt a chill, despite the humidity of the August night.

"Start… what, sweetheart?"

"The fire. Can I light it?"

"Why do you think there's going to be a fire? Come on now. Go back to bed. Want me to walk you home real quick?"

"I wanna start the *FIRE!*"

Harley jumped back. The last word was no hill. It was Everest. He was afraid, he realized. Afraid of a six-year-old girl. It was ridiculous. How could this kid want to burn down the courthouse? Kid probably didn't even know about the anarchists.

"Kids shouldn't start fires, honey. Just take Elroy and go on home. You live in that white house there?" he asked, pointing at a two-story brick home with four white columns standing sentinel along the broad front porch.

"You shouldn't ask little girls where they live, sir. Their parents might not like it. If you let me start the fire, I won't tell my parents you took me."

Alarm bells rattled Harley's head. There was something wrong with this kid. She'd just threatened him with a kidnapping charge… so that she could burn down a courthouse. It didn't make sense. Where was her innocence? Her sense of joy and wonder? Jackson would never talk this way. Of course, he'd been raised right.

"Give me the matches, sir."

"But—but why? Why do you want the matches? Tell me why. Please."

The girl took a step toward Harley. Harley retreated, trying not to recoil.

"Because Elroy and I don't like people who want to help black people."

Harley stood and stared at the girl, then at her turtle, who looked in the dark like he might be green.

"I can't let you do it, sweetheart," Harley said, barely above a whisper.

"I'm going to scream if you don't let me start the fire."

The girl meant it. If he gave her the matches, a six-year-old would start the fire that he had built. He would always know that. If he didn't give her the matches, she would scream, and then tell the police that Harley took her from her house. She was a bad kid. A bad seed, like in that old movie with another blond-headed girl.

His cell phone rang. He jumped again, then withdrew it with the hand that formerly held the gas can. Cannon Townsend's name lit up the screen.

"Cannon," Harley said with the phone to his right ear.

"What the hell are you doin' back there, Harley? We got twenty of us now. Things are still quiet 'cause of all the god-damn singin'. Effin' kumbaya, man. Where's the goddamn *fire*?"

"Sorry, man. There's a kid back here."

"A kid? At two fifteen in the effin' morning? No way. Just start the goddamn fire, dude."

"She—she wants to start it."

As Harley listened to Cannon Townsend rant about getting the job done and the need to get rid of the stupid kid, Harley looked at the girl.

"Why the hell does she want to start it, Harley?" Cannon's voice sounded with an incredulous tone.

Harley wasn't sure the girl had heard the question. "Sweetheart, why do you want to start the fire?"

The girl hugged Elroy to her left cheek and grinned.

"I wanna make the protesters look like bad guys."

Cannon exploded on the phone's speaker. "God damn it, Harley! I'm comin' back there. I'll light the match if you got it prepped. You take that little shit home where she belongs."

Harley had had several hot arguments with Cannon Townsend over the years. He'd lost all of them, at least by the opinions of those in the room.

"Sweetheart, let me take you home. You can't light a fire. That's bad. Don't you know it's bad to play with matches?"

The girl focused her eyes on Harley's. He looked away. They weren't the eyes of a six-year-old.

"I don't play with matches, sir. I play with bad men. I do what bad men do. Don't you know that, sir?"

"I'm not a bad man. Those people you hear out front are the bad people."

"I don't want to play with them. I want to play with *you*."

Harley wondered what happened to Cannon. If Cannon could just light the fire for him, Harley wouldn't be a bad man. The girl could play with Cannon instead. And Harley could go home and sit by his boy's bed. Maybe his fever had broken.

"Did Jackson die yet?"

The girl's face transformed into a smirk.

"*What* did you say?"

"You heard me, sir. Did Jackson die yet? You know, of the coronavirus?"

Harley stepped forward and gripped the girl by the ears. She laughed.

"How do you know Jackson? Tell me! You little—"

"We go to first grade together. Last week when I was almost better, I asked him if he wanted to put on my Star Wars mask.

He said he didn't get to have one because you said masks are for nancies. So I let him wear my mask for the rest of the day. He was very happy, sir."

Harley squeezed the girl's ears, to no effect. She should've been crying by now. Jackson had cried over far less.

The girl giggled. "They say it's like trying to breathe through jello, Mr. Francis."

"Who told you that? Who—who says that to a child?"

"My friend Pablo told me. Tomorrow you have to take Jackson to the hospital, sir. There's already jello in his lungs. Maybe the protesters put it there."

Rage burned in Harley's gut. If it weren't for the anarchists, he'd be home with his boy right this minute, tending to him. Surely the fever wasn't the coronavirus. Kids were fine with the coronavirus. That knowledge came straight from the president. The girl was just a psycho, trying to get a rise out of him. But why?

Cannon Townsend arrived, his pot belly heaving from the trek.

"Where's your commitment, man? Never mind," he said, ignoring the little girl's presence. "Just give me the matches. You've never really been a patriot anyway. And now Rowdy Smith tells me you can't even control your *wife?*"

For months Harley had taken abuse from Cannon at the Wednesday night meetings down at the First Baptist social hall. It would only get worse now that Rhonda was voting for Biden and letting the whole world know it. Worse, Harley feared that Rhonda would take Jackson to get tested for the covid tomorrow. She'd wanted to take him today when the fever spiked, but Harley had reminded her that if Jackson had to be hospitalized, they had no insurance. Rhonda agreed to wait and see, but if that fever wasn't gone by daylight, she was taking him straight to the hospital, coronavirus or no coronavirus. With Harley's luck, Jim Stephenson would be the ER doctor on duty. Might as well tell the whole militia that Harley Francis's son has the coronavirus. The only thing the militia hated more than anarchists and brown people was weakness. As Harley stood and stared at a man whose disapproval he'd feared since high school, he thought of his boy. He thought of his wife. He thought of this little girl who wanted to be the one to ignite the fire that would consume the courthouse and fuel the American division on which the president counted.

Cannon held out his left hand, palm up, then snapped his fingers. "Give me the effin' matches, Harley."

For the first time in his life, Harley Francis began to hate sickness. He wanted it to go away. He wanted to play hide and seek with Jackson, help him build that Lego Star Wars Millenium Falcon, the one still in the box from last Christmas. He wanted to make love with Rhonda for the first time in three weeks, and listen to the music she liked. And he wanted to kill Cannon Townsend.

What?

The girl was strangely quiet. She looked at Cannon, then at Harley.

"Here you go, sir," she said, and extended Elroy in his direction. "Take it. For Jackson."

"Give me the matches, moron," Cannon said. "We can't go to next-stage until this courthouse is on fire."

The girl ignored Cannon. "His temperature is a hundred and four, sir. Your wife's asleep. She stayed up as long as she could, hoping you could take over like she asked you to. And you're... here."

The girl had changed. Harley didn't know how a six-year-old kid could change in less than a minute, but the kid was different now. She knew. His boy was in big trouble, and she *knew*.

"Come with me," Harley said, accepting Elroy and reaching for her hand. The girl took it, her grip firmer than he'd thought she could muster.

"Where the *hell* are you *goin'*, Harley? We got work to do, you idiot."

"My boy's sick. I gotta go home."

"Give me the matches first, dick."

"No," Harley replied, surprised at the firmness in his voice. He unstrapped his AR-15 and pointed it at Cannon. "You're doing this without me. Dick. Find your own matches."

Cannon retreated a step. "If this goes wrong, I'm gonna tell the cops you set it." With that, Cannon turned and walked back in the direction of the protest, where the faint sound of singing continued to drift back toward the darkness.

Harley and the girl silently made their way along the service road to the Chamber of Commerce building, then advanced to the white Ram. Harley buckled the child into the front passenger seat, then circled around, climbed in and started the ignition. He sat for a moment.

"What's your name, sweetheart?" he asked, staring through the windshield toward the waving arms of the singing protesters.

"It's Mary, sir."

Harley handed Elroy to the girl.

"I want you to give Elroy to my boy, Mary. You've saved his life, I hope."

"And now you're saving mine, sir," the girl whispered. "You just don't know it yet."

***

On the Tuesday before Thanksgiving, a half day at Jackson's school, Harley and Rhonda Francis pulled up to Howerton Elementary School and dropped their boy off, thanking the teacher for her kindness in opening the Ram's rear door for their son. As they turned left on Argyle Boulevard to return home before Harley would head out to that patio project over in Tower Oaks, Rhonda said she couldn't wait until they could walk Jackson into school again.

"He loves his mask, though," Harley said, smiling.

Rhonda laughed. "He sure does. All four of them. We're keeping them when this is over, you know."

"Of course," Harley said, appreciating that good memories would still come from the coronavirus, because of it even, despite all the heartbreak.

"There will be other pandemics, they say," Rhonda said, soberness in her tone.

"Guess so," Harley said.

"Let's get four more, while we still can. Oh, and don't forget the ultrasound today. Two o'clock. I think it's gonna be a girl."

Harley reached his right hand to Rhonda's thigh and squeezed.

"What would we name her?"

Rhonda gripped Harley's hand, pressing it warmly against her leg.

"I'm thinking Mary," she said. "In honor of your vivid imagination."

KIDNAPPING
ROBERT E. LEE

✳ ✳ ✳

"It was Jack who came up with the idea to kidnap the general. Billy had nothing to do with it. All he did was, um, relieve himself on him. But everybody did that."

"So it was you and Jack Hudsall and Terrance Jackson. Nobody else participated in removing Robert E. Lee from the Kappa Alpha house on the night of April seventh?"

"That's right, sir. Just us three."

"Why do I get the feeling you're protecting Billy Oldenberg?"

"I'm not, sir. I recognize that relieving oneself on the portrait of Robert E. Lee is unacceptable. I'm sorry. But we did return him. Billy Oldenberg was only with us when we brought the general back."

"That was late at night on the ninth?"

"I think you know that, sir."

"Just answer the question, you little piece of shit."

"Okay. It was late at night on the ninth. The third day. The KAs that live at the house were drunk and asleep. All except for one."

"The one you think shot Billy Oldenberg?"

"The one who murdered Billy Oldenberg, yes."

"Listen, wiseass. This isn't a murder investigation. Chip Denton was standing his ground. This is South Carolina, boy. If you don't understand the law in South Carolina, you shouldn't go stealing property from other fraternity houses."

"We only borrowed him."

"And defaced him. Vandalized him. Dishonored his memory."

"I think the general took care of that last part all by himself, don't you, sir?"

"Keep talking smack, boy. The value of that portrait puts your crime in the category of felony theft. You ain't a kid no more, are you? You're nineteen. That's adult prison. The hard cases are gonna like you, Maurice."

"I don't go by Maurice. I go by Mo."

"Boy, let me ask you a question. Do I have a sign on my forehead that says 'Officer who gives a shit *what* you want people to call you'?"

"Chip Denton murdered my friend. We were just returning General Lee. Billy didn't even take part in borrowing him."

"Well, Maurice. Count yourself lucky. If Chip Denton really hated black people, he would've shot you and Terrance instead, now wouldn't he? When he stood his ground. But he shot the white Jewish guy. Now tell me. What happened to Billy's knife?"

"Billy didn't have a knife."

"Six people said he had a knife. Six eyewitnesses."

"That's bullshit, sir. The other drunk guys were asleep on the couches in the party room. Tyler shot Billy when we were hanging the general back up above the mantel. That's hardly stand your ground, sir."

"Don't tell me the law, boy. It was stand your ground. Or would you prefer I call it the Castle Doctrine?"

"I would prefer you understand that Billy Oldenberg was my friend."

"Then you shouldn't have stolen the general's portrait. Boy."

"Sir, are you trying to get a rise out of me? What, just because I'm black, you think I'm going to jump you for your racist bullshit? Give you an excuse to beat my face in? You forget this is a good school. I'm not stupid enough to let a campus cop goad me into teaching you a lesson. I'll take a lawyer now, please."

"We're just having a conversation, Maurice. I haven't read you your rights yet. Now tell me. When you stole General Lee, was it for the sole purpose of letting all eighty-nine members of the Sig Ep house relieve themselves on him for three days?"

"Absolutely, sir. And when we returned the general, Chip Denton murdered Billy for the sole purpose of showing the world that if you're a white guy helping black people, you'll get your ass shot by other white guys."

"Chip says you took his gun and hit him in the stomach."

"He'd just *shot* one of my best friends. Of course I took his—"

"That's assault, boy. Added to the theft charge, you're looking at fifteen years if you're sentenced consecutively. And you will be. Keep talking, why don't you."

"He was going to shoot Terrance and me too, officer. Don't you get that? *I* was standing *my* ground. Standing Terrance's ground too. Is it a crime to stand your ground while black in South Carolina?"

"Is it a crime to steal property from another fraternity house?"

"Not when that property is a symbol of treason and slavery and white supremacy and being proud of all three."

"I can see we're getting nowhere, Maurice. Let's shift gears. You want to go to prison for fifteen years, maybe more?"

"Not really."

"You bet your ass, not really. So tell me something, Maurice. Where was Jack Hudsall when you, Billy Oldenberg and Terrance Jackson were returning stolen property by illegally entering the KA house after two in the morning and scaring innocent people into defending themselves with deadly force?"

"Jack?"

"Yes, Jack. Where was he?"

"He—he was outside."

"Why was he outside, Maurice?"

"To make sure nobody walked in on us."

"So let me get this straight, Maurice. The white guy who dreamed up the idea of kidnapping Robert E. Lee got Billy Oldenberg to return the general with you two black guys. While Jack stayed outside to keep watch. Stand guard. That kind of thing?"

"Um... yes."

"So why wasn't he there when we got there? Our office is only a block from the KA house. I was on duty along with Tom Dancy, the uniform who got there first. No Jack Hudsall then. No Jack Hudsall now. Why?"

"Well. He..."

"Bet you feel pretty fucking stupid right now. Don't you, Maurice?

"Maurice? You awake, boy?"

"Yes, sir."

"Jack Hudsall was in his girlfriend's dorm room when our officer found him. They were, ah, amorously engaged at that precise moment. His girlfriend says he was with her since just after midnight. Sorry. Your pal didn't stick around. Wonder why."

"I—I don't know. Maybe—"

"Maybe you and Terrance *and* Billy took Bobby Lee from the get-go, Maurice. And maybe *you* shot Billy, not Chip. After all, your fingerprints are all over that gun, I'm willing to bet."

"But... the gunshot residue. It would be on—"

"You watch too much TV, boy. Chip's on his way to a family beach trip. Had to leave right after we questioned him. He said he does think it was an accident, you'll be happy to know. When you shot Billy while taking Chip's gun, that is. Chip won't be back in town till Monday."

"I *didn't*—wait, you let him *GO?*"

"Told him not to leave the state. He's a witness to a homicide, after all."

"I'd like a lawyer, please."

"Like I said, I haven't read you your rights. We're just chatting."

"You mean this isn't being recorded?"

"Just a bull session among friends. Now, you can sign a confession, or I can have an officer drive you and Terrance Jackson home and you can think about it until tomorrow. You live in the Sig Ep house, right? Over on Main Street? Maurice? I'm talking to you, boy."

"Yes. You know where it is."

"I sure do. So does Chief Denton. But he won't be back until Monday. The chief left me in charge till then. Okidoke, boy. I'll give you and Terrance that lift. Damn... will you just *look* at the time?"

A STUPID
ARGUMENT

✳   ✳   ✳

It was such a stupid argument.

The guy, *your friend*, thank you very much, wouldn't listen to what was real. He stands there at the party with his stupid Captain and Coke and pontificates about bad song lyrics. Like he's an expert or something. What I'm telling you is he doesn't know jack.

That's fine. Sure he's entitled. Problem is, he thinks he's entitled to be right about it. About everything. And everybody listens to him like he's right about everything. Ignoramus never heard of metaphors before, so he declares that a cake left out in the rain is the dumbest thing he's ever heard. He doesn't know jack.

I won't admit any such thing. It's been a long time since somebody stood up for what's right around that guy. For the love of God, it's not a stupid cake. It's *not a stupid cake.*

You know what? If I'm living in the past, what am I doing in this hospital room? Such a stupid argument, but did I start it? Did I? No need to answer that, because I know what you're going to say. But somebody has to stand up for what's right and beautiful and true in the world. Sometimes what's right and true and beautiful in the world is sadness. Everything ends up there. Everything. He doesn't get that because he doesn't know jack.

Fine. Sure. *I'm* the immature one. I wish you'd said that before I blew ten grand on your ring finger.

Yes. I said it. Blew. Speaking of sadness. But wait, I'm living
in the past again, aren't I? Here I get beaten to a pulp for standing up for what's right and true and beautiful in the world.
Present tense, sweetheart. But oh, I'm living in the past. Immature to boot. What about him? That asshat thinks he knows
everything. He wouldn't know sweet green icing if it fell on
him off a truck.

Maybe some pudding. Thanks, Nancy. Just put it on the tray.

Chocolate's great. No, not at all. You aren't interrupting
anything important. Is she, sweetheart?

I'll be fine. Going to sleep just as soon as my pleasant company leaves.

Absolutely will. Good night, Nancy.

I'm capable of a lot of things. Nice of you to notice one of them.

I'm not being sarcastic. I was complimenting your observa-
tory skills. So tell me. What do you like best about him?

Oh, come *on*. You know exactly about who. If I'm going to lie
here with one eye and three broken ribs, barely able to breathe
at all, I would like for you to share with me what's so special
about a man who doesn't care about metaphors and truth and
right and beautiful in this world.

Because metaphors are important! They're important! Why
can't you *see* that? Why can't you just appreciate that? Your
mind is so interested in trivial things, like—

Love? You say that word like I don't know what it is. I'm
the one in the hospital bed, aren't I? The song is *about* love, for
God's sake. He was so obtuse about it, about the lyrics, that I
can't believe you could stand there at the party and let his ignorance get the best of—

Well, yes, of course it's about lost love. That's what the
damned cake was. Past tense. So when the jackass laughed

about that, I had to give him that little poke in the chest. Just getting his attention about what's important. That's all.

I didn't say that.

No, I didn't. I said it was no fun being married to an uneducated *woman*, not, not... not what you said. I wouldn't say that. I would never say that. Not in those words.

Defending your honor! That's rich. He was defending your honor. That's really rich. Don't you understand that when *I* defended the most romantic song in the world, *I* was defending the very idea of you and me? That we need to bring the cake in from the rain now? Right *now?* What business was that of his? I was defending the metaphor that is you and me before the whole song becomes a metaphor *for* you and me. Know what I mean? Can you possibly grasp my meaning?

Don't say that. You're very intelligent. That's one of the reasons I married you.

Okay. So Carol Ann was also a very good reason. Yes. But I loved you then as I love you now. Even though you're ten thousand miles away, as it seems sometimes.

That's *exactly* my point. Carly Simon gets the metaphors too, for the same reasons. What is right and true and beautiful in the world.

All I did was poke him in the chest. Lightly. And he goes off on me. So here I lie, and you rub salt in the wound with your little digs about jackasses defending your honor.

Oh, for God's sake, donnez-moi une *break*, for once in my life. Carol Ann is old enough to know the difference. I trust that's why she isn't here.

Christ. Another swim meet? She should be entering the Junior Olympics at this rate. So now her father's in the hospital, her mother congratulates her father's attacker, and she's swimming the individual medley as we speak. So selfish. *Individual* medley. Talk about metaphors. Hand me that spoon, will you?

Okay. So enough about that. We're not getting anywhere. So what movies do they have for rent downstairs?

Why would you say something like that? Kramer Versus Kramer? Is that a joke?

But we're fighters, Elaine. We're fighters. Let's just get past this. Bring our cake in from the rain.

But I need you. Like the winter needs the spring.

For God's sake. America, honey. Hey! Where are you going? Please don't go. *Please.* Just turn around. I beg of you.

You see, it's like this. If you leave, at least in my lifetime I had one dream come true. I was blessed to be loved by someone as wonderful as—

No. K.C. and the Sunshine Band. You're thinking of Hutch. David Soul. They *got* it though, babe. They all got it. Unlike you and… what's-his-name.

Call me after the freestyle relay. That's the last event, right? Better yet, come back with Carol Ann and show me her ribbon. Yes, of course I forgive you, my love. I'll be counting the minutes and the hours.

Love you too, babe. Love you too.

Nancy? Nancy? *Nancy!*

Oh, thank heaven. I thought maybe your shift had ended without you saying goodbye.

She can't hear you, Nancy. She's gone. Gone to our daughter's swim meet. When she comes back with my daughter to show me her ribbons, can you send her right in?

You're very kind to say so. Indeed she is, Nancy. Indeed she is. Perhaps you might tell her that yourself some time. She could use the confidence. She takes after her mother that way.

Of course. I'll be happy to tell you when. I'll give you a signal so she doesn't know. I'll say "Vanilla today, thank you." That's your cue. She won't know I put you up to it.

So kind of you, Nancy. So kind.

Alexa… play 'MacArthur Park'.

Alexa. Stop. That's the Donna Summer version. You should know me better than that by now. Shouldn't you, darling?

QUESTIONS

✳ ✳ ✳

"**D**o I bore you?"

"Now why would you ask me something like that?"

"Why must you answer with a question, darling? Don't you know I hate that?"

"How am I supposed to know you hate that? Have I ever *told* you that you bore me?"

"Why do you think boredom is only indicated by a comment? Can't a person just observe clear signs of disinterest?"

"Like what? What signs of disinterest have I communicated to you? Have I yawned in your face? Ignored you? Rolled my eyes? Why do you have to read *into* things?"

"Read into things? You think I read into things when you stare at your freaking phone every time we eat? Why don't you like to dance anymore? Have real *conversations* anymore? Why don't you want to kiss me?"

"Would you like me to kiss you right now?"

"When have I *ever* asked you to kiss me, John? Why would I have needed to, when you used to kiss me just because you loved kissing me? Why don't you love kissing me anymore? Because I bore you? I'm not attractive to you now? Now that I'm forty? Or is there someone else again?"

"Jesus, you always have to do this, don't you? What is it about your martyrdom that isn't already sufficient? I'm here, aren't I? If I kiss you, deeply and passionately, right now, will you understand that you don't bore me? That there isn't someone else and there never was?"

"John, why can't you *listen* to yourself when you patronize me?"

"Oh, so now I'm patronizing you? Shouldn't you be careful in your choice of words? To patronize you wouldn't I at least have to be interested in you *and* your problems?"

"You hear that? *And* my problems? Can I lend you a mirror when you say that phrase? When I ask if I bore you, don't you ask yourself *why* I would ask that question? You just have to deflect, don't you? Want a shield for Christmas, darling?"

"Would that gift come with a little understanding? Understanding that a man who works sixty hours a week doesn't need this garbage two minutes after making himself a cocktail his wife *used* to have waiting for him?"

"Oh, so now I owe *you* an apology? For not having your special bourbon Manhattan all iced and cherried for you? What about your slippers and smoking jacket? What is this, nineteen-fifty-six? Don't you know I loved making you a Manhattan because I loved how you loved me? Because I loved how you came to my art openings with roses and kissed me in front of friends like you didn't care at all what other people think? What, becoming a market president for First American comes with a requirement that you only have one passion in life? Or was I right the first time? Is that it? That I'm old now, and it's time to think about trading in?"

"For God's sakes, Carrie, why would you make the ridiculous leap to—"

"Why did you *sleep* with her?"

"What? Who?"

"You think I don't have friends? Friends with cell phones? How was your little tryst with Marilyn at the Motel Six, John? Hello? Cat got your—"

"So if you knew, why wait two *months* to confront me, Carrie? Huh? I made one mistake, two months ago, and to spare your feelings I never told you because of my shame and regret, and now you tell me you've had friends *spying* on me?"

"*How* is a friend spotting you coming out of a motel room with Marilyn Carter a case of spying, John? She took a picture and sent it to me, and then what, somehow that makes me guilty of mistrust and espionage? You *did it,* and yet you dare to deflect guilt back on me yet again? How dare you?"

"Okay, now, can you just—just put that thing away? Why do you need props for your drama? It's not loaded, is it?"

"You think this is a prop, you bastard? Can you tell me this? What would Marilyn Carter do with this prop if she were standing here right now? Did she *really* take her own life, John? You're the only one who knows, aren't you?"

"Can you just put that down so we can talk? Don't you know I love you? Don't you know that, baby?"

"And how would I 'know that' when you just had to go embarrass both of us, with Marilyn Carter enthusiastically helping you do it?"

"Well, Carrie, she *is* dead, isn't she? Don't you see? Don't you see that I made my choice? Don't you see that I *chose* you?"

"Oh? And how would I see that?"

"You don't see that she had plenty to live for? That she was twenty-seven years old, her whole life in front of her? Why would she take a leap off her balcony?"

"You—you mean you... pushed her?"

"Don't you know that I love you?"

"You *pushed* her?"

"Now why on earth would I do that, darling?"

"Can you back up a little? John? Can you *please back up*?"

"Why would I want to back up when I want to kiss you so passionately? When I want to have deep conversations with you? When I want to make both our special cocktails every single night? Why would I not want to move forward with you, when we can leave this world together?"

"Leave this world together? John—will you please stop? Please?"

"Is that my gun? Did you… check the chamber, Carrie?"

"Do you really want to find out?"

"Looks like I have to give you the same ride I gave Marilyn, don't I, Carrie? Now why don't you calm down and *give me the goddamned*—"

***

"Mrs. Marbury?"

"Yes, officer?"

"Where is that cell phone, so we can view the video?"

"Um… see it there? On top of the balcony wall? Leaning against the Heineken? Oh, and officer?"

"Yes, ma'am?"

"When you watch it, can you turn up the volume?"